I.S. 61 Library

Bay Girl

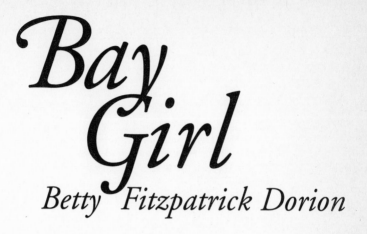

Betty Fitzpatrick Dorion

COTEAU BOOKS

Edited by Barbara Sapergia.

Cover painting by Janet Wilson.
Cover and book design by Duncan Campbell.
Printed and bound in Canada.

The publisher gratefully acknowledges the financial assistance of the Saskatchewan Arts Board, the Canada Council for the Arts, the Department of Canadian Heritage, and the City of Regina Arts Commission, for its publishing program.

Coteau Books celebrates the 50th Anniversary of the Saskatchewan Arts Board with this publication.

Canadian Cataloguing in Publication Data

Betty Dorion, 1952-
Bay girl
ISBN 1-55050-132-1

I. Title.

PS8557.07473B38 1998   jC813'.54   C98-920118-X
PZ7.D72758Ba 1998

COTEAU BOOKS
401-2206 Dewdney Ave.
Regina, Saskatchewan
Canada   S4R 1H3

AVAILABLE IN THE US FROM
General Distribution Services
85 River Rock Drive, Suite 202
Buffalo, New York, USA 14207

CONTENTS

For Mom, Aunt Dora, Aunt Moira,
Aunt Florie, and Uncle Nash.

And in loving memory of Gran,
Aunt Martha, Aunt Bessie,
and Uncle Willy.

1. Gran's Letter

"Look, Jeanette, how clear the harbour is!"

For a split second Jeanette looked.

That was all Patsy needed. Her fingertips winged her best friend's shoulder. "Last touch!" she called, laughing.

"No fair, Pats!" Jeanette howled, lunging after her.

Patsy grabbed her school bag from the ground and skedaddled out of reach of Jeanette's long arm. She ran a safe distance up the steep lane and then turned to wave to her friend, who lived a bit farther along the shore.

They played this game every day after school, and this time Patsy won. Even if it was by a trick. A clear day in Cape Grande! No wonder Jeanette looked! It didn't happen that often. Patsy could see every house around the shore and below them the fish stages, perched right on the edge of the Atlantic Ocean.

Grinning at the trick she'd played on her best friend, Patsy darted up the lane and around the corner of the house. Through the kitchen window, she spotted her aunt sitting at the end of the table.

"What's Aunt Dora doing here this time of day?"

The porch door slammed behind her. Book bag and sneakers found a place in the corner and the raincoat she'd left at school yesterday managed to land on a hook behind the door.

Her presence already announced, Patsy barged into the kitchen. "Hi, Aunt Dora," she said, letting the door swing wide. "I didn't expect to see you here." She gave her aunt a warm smile. "Where's Florence Anne?"

Aunt Dora returned the smile, but it wasn't her usual cheery one. "Hello, dear," she said. "The baby's home with her dad. Having a nap, the two of them." That was it. Not one story about what Florence Anne had gotten into that day.

But at least Aunt Dora had said hello. Mom sat sideways at the table with her feet crossed at the ankles. She didn't look up from the letter in her hand. One foot diddled nervously against the chair leg. Her old beige canvas slippers had seen better days. Patsy had long ago given up trying to get her to buy fluffy ones. There was nothing fluffy about Mom.

"Who's the letter from, Mom?"

No reply. Hunched over the page, Mom seemed to be reading the same part over and over.

"From Gran," Aunt Dora said. She tugged a tissue from her sweater pocket and wiped her eyes behind her glasses.

Something was wrong. Patsy could feel it. And the doleful look on Aunt Dora's face proved it.

Gran lived farther along the coast in Shoal Harbour, Fortune Bay. Uncle Wish lived with her; he hadn't married. Something must have happened. But if Gran were sick, or hurt, she probably wouldn't be able to write a letter. Had something happened to Uncle Wish?

Patsy hoped with all her heart that Uncle was all right. She wished someone would tell her what was going on. Whatever it was must be awful to make Aunt Dora look like that. Her cup of tea sat in front of her full to the brim. And she hadn't touched the slice of banana bread on her plate. Hadn't buttered it either.

Aunt Dora loved to eat, especially Mom's baking. She went on diets, but she cheated so much she never lost much weight. She used to belong to a diet club and starved herself the Wednesday members weighed each other. Then she'd stop at Patsy's house on the way home and have a night lunch, laughing with every bite she took!

Aunt Dora wasn't laughing today. Or eating.

Patsy peered over Mom's shoulder. She squinted with the effort of trying to decipher her grandmother's handwriting, but could make out only a word here and there. "What's wrong, Mom?" she asked, looking from the letter to her mother's distressed face.

Mom read on to the next page as if she hadn't heard Patsy. She rubbed her finger back and forth over the spot on her temple that was still red from the Toni perm she'd gotten a couple of days ago.

Patsy was miffed. The least Mom could do was let her know what was going on. It was her business too. The letter was from her Gran. She clenched her teeth, sucked in a loud hissy breath, and shook Mom's shoulder.

Finally Mom stirred. She had the distracted look of

someone coming out of a daze. "Shoal Harbour is being resettled," she said. The words sounded hollow, as if Mom couldn't bring herself to feel their meaning. Looking past Patsy, she stared out the window at the harbour.

Patsy planted herself in Mom's face. "What are you talking about?" she asked, hands on her hips. "What does resettled mean?"

Aunt Dora, always the calmer of the two, answered Patsy. "Resettlement means the government is closing down the outports and moving all the people out."

Patsy puckered her brows in disbelief. She ignored the long bangs sticking in her eyes. "What?" She looked from Mom to Aunt Dora. How could they move a whole place? She didn't understand. "Everyone? Gran and Uncle Wish too? Why?"

Mom's mind was back from whatever distant place it had been. "Yes, Patsy, yes," she said. "Shoal Harbour. The whole place. Gran and Uncle Wish too." Impatience with Patsy's questions was a sign of how upset she was.

Aunt Dora twisted the tissue in her hand. "Well, Mae," she said, "if she has to leave home, it'll be the end of her." She sighed heavily. "She'll be gone within the year, to be sure."

Patsy tensed at the tremor in Aunt Dora's voice. Did Aunt Dora mean that Gran would die? Stunned to silence, she watched her aunt trace the outline of a flower on the patterned oilcloth that covered the table. The clock ticked louder than ever on top of the wood and oil stove.

Patsy tried to make some sense of what she'd heard.

"Why does the government want to resettle Shoal Harbour?"

Aunt Dora picked up her cold tea and set it down again. "Who knows why they do a lot of things?" she said, more to herself than to Patsy. "There's been talk of it for a while, but no one thought they'd go ahead with it."

Mom roused up in anger. "Sleeveens is what they are, the whole lot of them." She raged on. "For God's sake, the outports are the backbone of Newfoundland. Fishing is our life."

Patsy put her arm around Mom's rigid shoulder. "How come they're doing this?" she asked.

Aunt Dora answered her. "They say it costs too much to look after all the small outports along the coast." Her voice ridiculed the government and its policy.

Mom pulled Patsy down onto her lap. Normally Patsy would have none of that. She was definitely too old for lap sitting. But this time she endured it. She even let Mom brush her bangs out of her eyes.

Aunt Dora explained. "They say that if people moved to larger places they could have better education, roads, hospitals, and whatever else."

This idea infuriated Mom. Patsy felt her bristle. "Bloody nonsense!" Mom fair spat the words. Patsy had the feeling that if one of the government men were here right now Mom would shake the stuffing out of him like she was shaking the letter in her hand. "And what about the dollars they'll spend to do all this?" Mom didn't wait for a reply. "If they used the money in a proper way in the first place, there'd be enough to look after the outports." She shook her head in disgust. "The old people will never make it," she said. "They'll never survive."

Nudging Patsy off her knee, she scanned the letter again and read the last few lines aloud. "It don't matter about me. I'm old. It's Wish I'm worried about. Having to pack up and move will be awful hard on him."

Strong feelings cracked Mom's words and scared Patsy. She watched Mom run her hand back and forth over the wrinkles Patsy had made in her cotton housedress.

"Why will moving be so hard on Uncle Wish?" Patsy asked, in a small, tight voice.

Mom twitched impatiently. "Patsy, you wouldn't understand."

Aunt Dora took Patsy's hand. "Wish lived all his life in Shoal Harbour." She looked at Mom. "Sure, he hardly ever left, did he, except for the week he spent here a few summers ago?"

Mom stared out the window, her eyes shiny with tears. "And he couldn't wait to get back home again. Right lost he was without his boat and his nets." She passed the letter back to her sister. "Dora," she said, "we'll just have to go see what we can do."

Aunt Dora nodded. She read the letter through one more time.

Patsy hopped up on the counter next to Aunt Dora's chair, something Mom never let her do. Now she didn't even seem to notice. "What will they do with all the buildings?" she asked.

"God knows," Mom said. "Leave them to rot, I suppose."

"Will Gran and Uncle Wish move here?"

"Now, Patsy, don't start with your questions. We'll just have to wait and see."

Aunt Dora stood up to go. She pulled her blouse down over her stretchy black pants.

Aunt Dora always wore pants. And Mom always wore dresses and skirts, except when she went berry picking. Patsy was like Aunt Dora. She liked pants best.

"I'll talk to Jose," Aunt Dora said, "and I'll let you know." She tucked the letter into her pocket. "I'll have to take the baby."

Mom nodded. She uncrossed her bare white legs and stood up. The only sun Mom's legs ever saw was a beam on the kitchen floor. She always wore stockings outdoors but took them off the minute she came inside.

Patsy hugged Mom's considerably browner arm. "Are we going to Shoal Harbour?" In her excitement she forgot about not asking questions.

Mom didn't answer. Patsy was used to that. Mom was slow with answers.

Patsy had never been to the tiny fishing village in Fortune Bay where Mom and Aunt Dora had grown up. But Mom had told her lots of stories of how her grandfather had skippered a fishing vessel that traveled to places like Boston, the Labrador Coast, and the French islands of St. Pierre and Miquelon, and how he'd brought home gifts from his voyages. It had sounded so exciting! And now she might get to go there!

Patsy didn't really understand what Mom and Aunt Dora were so upset about. She'd love to have Gran and

Uncle Wish live near them.

Patsy had never met her grandmother, but she felt she knew her. There was a snap of Gran on the mantel in the front room. She wore a black dress, gold wire-rimmed glasses, and a smile like Aunt Dora's. Gran always sent presents at Christmas and never forgot Patsy's birthday.

Gran wouldn't die when she saw how happy the whole family would be to have her and Uncle Wish near.

And maybe Uncle Wish could take Patsy fishing. She loved boats. Mom said it was in her blood. She didn't get to go in one very often though. Patsy's dad was dead; he had died of tuberculosis when she was only two. And she seldom saw her only brother, who worked on a fishing dragger in Nova Scotia.

Sometimes Jeanette's dad, who was a fisherman too, took them out in the harbour when he wasn't too busy.

Mom walked Aunt Dora to the door. Patsy slipped past them. She skipped around to the front of the house, climbed up on the verandah, and perched on the railing.

At the bottom of the lane, a strip of salt-eaten pavement curved along the shore, like a washed-out grey stripe around the rim of a bowl. There were no sidewalks like St. John's had, just brown dirt that was always eroding down the bank in the rain. Patsy watched two cars pass with barely enough room to stay on the road.

Her gaze wandered across the strand and past the causeway to the harbour. The water was perfect, steeped in sky blue with sunny sparkles skittering over the surface. And not a trace of fog. Not even around the Cape.

The familiar scattering of punts and dories and skiffs on their moorings lured a dreamy smile to her mouth. She thought about Uncle Wish and his boat. As clear as her grand view of the Cape, Patsy saw herself and Jeanette rowing Uncle's dory, pulling into shore now and then to give a friend from their class a harbour tour.

In the distance the Point and the Cape loomed rocky and solid on either side of the harbour entrance. Through the narrow channel, Patsy glimpsed the sweep of ocean beyond. Would Gran and Uncle Wish arrive that way? Would they steam into the harbour on a coastal boat if they came?

Anticipation rippled up her back and soused her skin with delightful shivers. She leapt off the railing and streaked inside. "Are we going?"

Mom threw out the cold tea and set the cups in the sink. Her mind must have been far away again. She never left dirty dishes in the sink, ever.

"I don't want you to say anything about it, not a word, mind you, until Dora talks to Jose," Mom said, in a no-nonsense tone. "We'll just have to wait and see."

For Patsy, that was the hardest thing in the world.

2. Patsy's News

"Mom, can I stay at Jeanette's house tonight when you go to work? Mrs. Eileen said I can stay there any time. As long as it's all right with you."

"I s'pose. Just make sure you and Jeanette do your homework. The show should be over by ten o'clock." Patsy was surprised when Mom gave in right away. She'd been prepared to nag a bit.

Usually, when Mom went to work at the movie theatre Patsy went to Aunt Moira's, just down the lane. She loved staying at Auntie's, where there was a whole crowd of cousins to carry on with. But tonight she had big things to talk about with Jeanette.

"See-ya," she yelled to Mom. She grabbed her book bag from the corner and didn't stop running until she arrived at Jeanette's back porch. She popped her head in the kitchen door. "Guess what!"

Jeanette was drying dishes with several of her brothers and sisters underfoot. She struggled with an oversized pot. "Just a minute," she said, and flashed Patsy a wide smile. "I'm almost done and then we can talk out on the steps."

"Okay," Patsy nodded. "I'll wait out here for you."

Jeanette joined her in no more than two minutes, easing the door shut to avoid catching baby Angela's fingers. She tugged her rolled-up sleeves down over her freckled arms.

Patsy didn't give Jeanette a chance to guess, or to say anything at all. "We're going to Shoal Harbour!" she squealed.

Jeanette scrunched up her face until her green eyes all but disappeared. "Where?"

"Shoal Harbour...where Gran and Uncle Wish live. Uncle Wish has a boat and I'll get to go out in it."

Jeanette caught her wavy mop of brown hair in her hands like she was struggling with a ponytail. She dropped it down her back. "When are you going?"

"I'm not sure yet. Mom has to talk to Aunt Dora. Probably next week."

"Next week!" Jeanette squawked, a woebegone look on her freckled face. "Right when our holidays start! What kind of a summer will it be if you're going away?"

"I won't be gone long," Patsy assured her best friend, "and when I come back Gran and Uncle Wish will probably be with us, and we'll be able to go out in Uncle Wish's boat." Patsy flicked her shoulder-length plaits off her neck. Mom always tied them with stiff ironed ribbons and they always scratched. "I'll ask him to teach us to row," she added.

Jeanette arched a thick eyebrow. Her face didn't look quite so forlorn.

Patsy sensed a stir of interest.

"Do you think he'll let me row too?" Jeanette asked.

There was a definite gleam in her eyes.

"I'll ask him when I go to Shoal Harbour, but I'm sure he will," Patsy assured her friend.

Her excitement caught in her chest for a jiffy. She wasn't one hundred percent sure that they were going to Shoal Harbour, though they probably would, she told herself. And Uncle Wish and Gran would probably come home with them. Where else could they go? Like a small fish bone that gets stuck in the throat on the way down and a good swallow sends it on its way, Patsy put the "probablies" out of her mind.

Darkness and the damp sea air sent them inside and homework kept them busy for the next while. Every few minutes Patsy pulled the print curtains aside to check for Mom. Close to ten o'clock she spotted her mother striding over the road and hightailed it out the door to meet her. She didn't want Mom chatting with Mrs. Eileen tonight, just in case Jeanette's mom had heard them talking. When Patsy's mother said to keep quiet about something, she meant it.

The next morning in the schoolyard Jeanette announced to Stella and Carmee, "Patsy's going away for a holiday."

Too late Patsy realized she should have had Jeanette promise not to tell. The pleasure of bragging couldn't stifle the guilt she felt.

"Where're you going?" asked Stella, in the stuck-up voice that matched her stuck-up self. Usually she was the only one who went away on holidays.

Patsy stammered, "We might be going to Shoal Harbour."

Stella was point blank. "And you might not?"

Patsy's brown eyes blazed. "No, we're going for sure. But I don't know exactly when. Mom has to talk to Aunt Dora."

"Oh," said Stella, flicking her ponytail. "Where is Shoal Harbour anyway?"

"In Fortune Bay," Patsy told her. "Everybody knows that."

Carmee gave Stella a dirty look. "What difference is it where Shoal Harbour is?" she said. "At least Patsy's going somewhere." Carmee loved putting Stella in her place. Now she looked at Patsy, a satisfied smile on her face. "Right, Patsy?"

Stella shut her mouth.

Jeanette relished giving Stella all the exciting details. "Yeah, and her Gran and Uncle Wish are coming to live here, and Uncle Wish has a boat that Patsy can use any time she wants."

Patsy wished Jeanette wasn't such a good friend. Mom would be rory-eyed if she knew what Patsy's mouth was up to. She'd say that Patsy had no business telling anyone, not even Jeanette. But how could she keep anything this good from her best friend?

The bell rang. They edged toward the door with the little group still listening to Patsy explaining resettlement. All except Stella.

"You mean there won't be a single soul left there?" Carmee asked.

"Not one," Patsy replied, "and the houses and

everything will be left to rot."

"Just like a ghost town," said Carmee, whose whole family stayed up late watching westerns on their new television.

Sister Damien, their teacher, called from the classroom doorway. "Come girls. Summer holidays are still a week away."

"Let's tell Sister, Patsy." Carmee didn't wait for an answer. Not allowed to run in the corridor, she skated on the gleaming hardwood floor till she reached Sister Damien. "Sister," she said, "Patsy's going away for a holiday." She swung around. "Where to, Pats?"

"Shoal Harbour," Patsy told Sister, feeling shy, and sorry she had such a big mouth.

"How lovely, Patsy!" Sister said. "Do you have relatives in Shoal Harbour?"

"My grandmother and uncle," Patsy replied.

Jeanette chimed in, "And they're coming to live here, and Patsy's uncle has a boat, and Patsy can use it any time she wants."

Sister smiled and shooed them into the classroom.

Patsy's insides churned. What if they didn't go? How would she live it down? Next to her own, Jeanette's mouth was the biggest in Cape Grande. Well, Stella's was pretty big too, she giggled to herself.

Patsy put in a long guilt-ridden morning. She checked with Mom at noon. "Was Aunt Dora here yet?"

No luck.

The afternoon in school was even longer. She read a note from Carmee.

Dear Patsy,
You're sure lucky to be going away for a holi-
day. When is your Uncle Wish coming? Do
you think I'll be able to have a boat ride?
Carmee

Notes from three other girls, Sue, Alice, and Beverly followed. She answered each with a forced smile and a half-hearted nod of her head.

At three-thirty Patsy bolted out the door with the sound of the bell still in her ears. Her feet pounded down Church Lane. She managed to dodge the pot-holes, and there were lots of them. Around the shore she ran, slowing only to swing her book bag to the other hand to even out the bumping against her legs.

Eyes peeled for any sign of Aunt Dora, she ran right to the porch door. No wonder she was as skinny as an eel, Mom often said. Patsy never walked when she could run. Except for church – there her mother forced her to walk.

In the doorway she caught her breath at the sound of a baby's squeal. She dropped her ton of books in the porch. Aunt Dora was here!

Before she was in the door her words were halfway out. "Are we going?"

Mom looked at the clock. "You're home fast." She planted a kiss on the top of Patsy's dark head. "Running again, I s'pose."

Aunt Dora gave her an affectionate grin. "That's so she won't miss anything," she said.

Patsy ignored their comments. "Are we going?" she asked again, trying to read Mom's face.

Mom said nothing.

"Yay," Patsy cheered, "yay!" This was as close to a yes as she would get from Mom, who was a little on the cautious side.

One-year-old Florence Anne, on the floor, bounced up and down on her round diapered bottom. She raised her arms to be carried, loving every minute of the fuss Patsy had created.

Holding her, Patsy danced around the kitchen until she and the baby were dizzy. They collapsed in fits of giggles into the armchair.

A good part of Patsy's lightheartedness was relief. In her mind's eye she saw herself, face red as a lobster, if she'd had to tell her friends the trip was off. She'd have left town on the first steamer.

She felt like a blister in her soul had been burst with this news, and the guilt flowed out of her in a deep sigh. She listened to her mother and Aunt Dora discussing details. "...St. Bernard's...best place to catch the boat." The baby slapped at her face, wanting to play again. Patsy tried to shush her. They would have to go by boat. She'd never been on a big steamer before!

Florence Anne, restless now, wriggled out of Patsy's arms and slid down to the floor.

Aunt Dora said, "I phoned St. Bernard's. There's a coastal boat due in next Friday at eleven o'clock. If we take that one, we can be in Shoal Harbour by four."

Mom nodded. "I'll write tonight and tell Mom and Wish we're coming."

Patsy jumped up. She had to go tell Jeanette.

3. The Burgeo

"No, Patsy, there's no time to go see Jeanette. Jose'll be here any minute."

"I just want to say good-bye," Patsy pleaded.

"You said good-bye last night," Mom said. "Jeanette isn't even up yet. It's only quarter to eight. Now set the suitcases out on the step."

Patsy had just laid the second suitcase down when Uncle Jose's dusty green Ford pulled to a stop at the bottom of the lane. Mom checked the water faucet and stove for the hundredth time while Uncle Jose stowed the luggage in the trunk.

Patsy hopped into the back seat and slid across to sit next to the window. Mom settled next to her and held out her arms to Florence Anne, who was putting up a noisy fuss to join the action in the back. But when the baby saw her father sit behind the wheel and fiddle with the radio dials, she decided the front was the place to be and was soon back in Aunt Dora's restraining arms.

Aunt Dora's voice rose steadily higher amid all the

racket until Uncle Jose began to sing his version of "Lots o' fish in Bonavist Harbour." It was the only song Patsy had ever heard him sing, and he always sang the same verse over and over. Everyone settled down after that, even the baby.

After one left turn, they were on the only road out of Cape Grande, uphill all the way. Patsy looked out the window. The small community below was bordered by two main roads, one that ran in a horseshoe around the harbour and another parallel to it at the top of the hill. In between, box-shaped houses and bungalows grabbed onto the hillside, sometimes at odd angles. And often odd colours. Patsy hated the kelp green of Teresa Beck's house, but she loved the dandelion yellow of her friend Beverly's house.

Right away Patsy spotted Jeanette's blue bungalow close to the bottom road, then Auntie's grey two-story, and her own white house up the lane. Her eyes wandered to the Cape at the entrance to the harbour, its mid-section cut off in early morning fog. The tip looked like it floated free in the sky. After a dip in the road the whole harbour was lost to view.

Patsy traced their route on a map. Up and down hills, alongside ponds and marshes they drove, past rock-capped ridges, heaps of them, and the odd clump of stunted spruce. A few times they drove right through a sheer rock mountain, its middle dynamited away, Uncle Jose said. Patsy craned her neck to see the tops of the granite walls that rose straight up on either side of the road.

Once in a while the bumpy, pot-holed, dirt highway cut through a small town. But best of all were the times it followed the curve of a cove or bay. Patsy wished she could run into the shallows and wash away the dust and grit that sifted in from the dirt highway. She tried to count the boats on their moorings. Once she counted fourteen before they rounded a turn and left boats and bay behind.

"It's just around the bend now," Uncle Jose announced. He started to sing "Lots o' fish...."

Patsy couldn't sit another minute. She bounced on the seat as she sang along, all the while keeping her eyes peeled for the Burgeo. "There it is!" she squealed, lunging over the front seat to point.

Florence Anne shrieked with delight and stiffened in her mother's arms, demanding to be released.

Patsy felt Mom yank at her shirt. "Patsy, sit down, will you? You're going to make Jose have an accident carrying on like that."

Aunt Dora rubbed her collarbone. "I'll be black-and-blue by the time we get there."

A chuckle from Uncle Jose. He reached over and patted Florence Anne's fair head.

They drove right to the government wharf. Good thing it wasn't far, because seeing the Burgeo so close took Patsy's breath away. And it didn't come back until she hopped out of the car onto the wharf and was hit smack in the face with a blast of salty sea air.

What a size the Burgeo was! It hadn't looked that big sailing into the harbour at home. But then she'd never been this close.

While the grownups unloaded the luggage, Patsy sized up the coastal boat. Steamers like this were the main link between outports, especially the more isolated ones, and the rest of Newfoundland. They sailed the coast year-long, picking up and delivering mail, cargo, and relatives.

Already on the far end of the wharf there were piles of freight – lumber, drums, barrels, all sizes of wooden crates, and more were being lowered over the hull of the ship down to the wharf.

In some places there was reddish-brown rust on the black hull, but the top part of the steamer was all white. That must be where the captain and crew's living quarters and the cabins were, Patsy decided. There was even a cafeteria, Mom had said. Patsy couldn't wait to board!

How would they get aboard anyway? She looked and looked, but couldn't see any steps. Not even a gangplank. Wait a minute. Was that it? Oh, no. Patsy's heart dropped like the dead weight of an anchor.

A terrifying step-like contraption was being lowered from the deck of the steamer. The breeze off the harbour lifted it like a kite. It swung crazily about in the air before a dockhand reined it in and the metal walkway settled on the wharf.

Mom and Aunt Dora were busy saying good-bye to Uncle Jose and didn't notice the flimsy thing. It had no railings, just rope on either side that swayed back and forth in the breeze. Sickening.

Patsy's eyes zeroed in on the landing hanging out over the harbour depths with nothing under it but the deep Atlantic. Terror squelched every ounce of excitement. She saw herself tumbling under the rope railing. Her mind shrieked, "I'm not getting on this boat!"

Nobody heard.

Passengers edged closer to the steps. Patsy scuffed

along behind Mom. It had been a few years since she'd held Mom's hand in public. And she hadn't planned on embarrassing herself by doing so. But that was before. When Mom set foot on the first step, Patsy grabbed her arm. When Mom moved to the second step, Patsy's feet stayed planted on the wharf.

"The young'un seems a mite scared," rumbled a deep voice behind her.

Patsy glared up into a bristly, grinning face. She was in no mood to be teased; her look made that plain.

Mom stopped talking to Aunt Dora and finally looked at Patsy. However, before Mom could say a word, the dockhand leaned toward Patsy, bringing with him some ripe odours, among them the strong stink of tobacco. Patsy cringed.

His Popeye arms shot out, surrounded her, and hoisted her off her feet. Too shocked to make a sound of protest, she gasped and lost her grip on Mom's hand. Stunned though she was, Patsy was keenly aware of Florence Anne's solemn stare.

In view of the whole wharf, the dockhand, with Patsy held high, slipped past Mom and Aunt Dora and skipped up the steps, metal clanging behind him. He didn't even hold the ropes.

Patsy had never been on a roller coaster, but her stomach had a ride of its very own on the short trip to the deck of the Burgeo. Her heart also wanted no part of this experience. It had moved up to her throat and was thumping out of her body. When the landing shook under the seamen's dirty rubber boots, she shut her eyes, dizzy with fear.

He plopped her down on the deck like a sack of

flour, tweaked her plait, and whistled his way back down to the wharf.

Patsy's knees wobbled, jellyfish-weak. When her insides settled, she surveyed the deck. No one had witnessed the mortifying scene. She tucked in her white shirt and strolled along the safe, enclosed railing of the Burgeo, her face the colour of her new red pants.

The cool breeze off the harbour patted her cheeks like a damp cloth. Overhead, seagulls screamed. She watched them patrol the waterfront. One of the boldest perched on the railing just out of reach before swooping down to the wharf.

She spied Mom with Aunt Dora and the baby, about halfway up to the deck. Mom chatted to Aunt Dora and didn't look the least bit anxious about Patsy. In her mind, Patsy told her mother off.

The women stepped onto the deck and looked at her with knowing smiles.

Patsy looked away, pretending not to see them.

However, she forgot her anger as the Burgeo prepared to sail. Patsy watched the deck hands raise the metal steps and secure them. Then, freed at last from the stout ropes, the Burgeo's horn blew two short blasts.

Florence Anne, in Aunt Dora's arms, jumped at the sudden noise.

Patsy laughed. "That means we're leaving!" she told her little cousin. "Let's wave to everyone!" She took the baby's hand and they waved to people milling about on the wharf.

The steamer backed away from the dock, cutting a wide arc in the harbour. Patsy left Mom and Aunt

Dora at the railing and raced the length of the deck so she could see the water churning in the Burgeo's wake.

"Patsy, come back here," Mom called, using her going-to-work stride to catch up. "You can't go running all over the place here. It's too dangerous."

"I'll be careful," Patsy promised, and headed forward again. She stopped about halfway so that she could see the little town grow smaller with distance and still view the open sea as they neared the last headland.

Once they lost sight of land, Patsy was content to look for the cafeteria. She peered through portholes and jumped through the hatches. She liked the rolling motion of the steamer as they stood in line to choose sandwiches, and laughed when she lost her balance and had to grab a railing for support.

"Haven't got your sea legs yet, eh?" teased the man behind them.

"Wait till we get out in the bay," Aunt Dora laughed.

"Why?" Patsy wanted to know.

"The sea always gets heavier," Mom said. "I hope you don't get sick."

About twenty minutes later Patsy knew what Mom meant. She laid her glass down and the table seemed to come up to meet it. Patsy giggled. It was a challenge to stand up without holding on to something, but she was determined to get her sea legs.

"Let's go see the waves," she begged.

Mom and Aunt Dora were busy chatting with the other passengers. "Those are only whitecaps," Mom said. "If there were waves you'd know it!"

"Can I go by myself? I'll be careful, promise."

Mom hesitated.

"Let her go, Mae," Aunt Dora said. "There's enough out there to watch out for her."

Mom nodded. "We'll be along as soon as Dora changes the baby."

Patsy, legs unsteady, strode out on deck and into the breeze, which had picked up considerably since they'd gone inside. Mom and Aunt Dora hadn't been grum at all since they'd boarded the Burgeo. Patsy was glad.

She chose a spot forward, leaned her head on her arms, and let the wind whip her hair around.

Soon she felt another tug. Florence Anne, in Mom's arms, had plucked a ribbon off her plait and held it high. The baby laughed when the wind tried to wrench it away from her.

Just then a woman next to Aunt Dora sighted land. Patsy was disapointed. She wanted to be the first to see Shoal Harbour. "Are we there?" she asked.

"Not yet. Not for close to an hour," Mom replied. "That's the coastline you see." The eagerness in Mom's voice was sweet to Patsy's ears.

She glued her eyes to the distant shore. For a long time they sailed past deep inlets and rocky cliffs. Then the Burgeo made a wide turn. Patsy's breath quickened. This must be it! "Are we there?" she asked again.

This time Mom said yes! Patsy felt the steamer cut back its engines. She would have liked to speed up! The Burgeo, in no particular hurry, rounded a high craggy bluff jutting out into the bay.

Hidden behind it was Shoal Harbour.

4. Shoal Harbour

Patsy nudged Mom. "Look at those houses! See how close they are to the water?"

At home houses were near the water too, but not like this. Patsy spied a pretty pink one with white trim. It was practically in the landwash. Others, scattered behind and between rocks and hills, made her think of bright beads busted loose from a string – a red one here, a blue one there, while the rest of the colourful chain fell carelessly along either side of the single, narrow dirt road.

The Burgeo maneuvered in slow motion until finally it was next to the wharf. "What's taking so long?" Patsy asked, hopping from one foot to the other. At least fifteen more minutes went by before the metal gangway was lowered.

"How come there're so many people on the wharf?"

Mom replied, "Pretty well anyone who can walk comes down when the steamer docks."

"We don't do that back home."

"Patsy, that's because we don't have to wait a whole week, or two, for the coastal boat to bring the mail and everything else we need. If we can't get something in the shops home, we can just hop in a car and go to Marystown." Mom lowered her voice. "See that woman Aunt Dora is talking to?"

Patsy nodded.

"Well, she told me she's on her way to Belleoram to see the doctor. She has a cousin here in Shoal Harbour, she said, so she's going ashore to visit her on the wharf while the Burgeo is docked."

Mom's voice rose then, and she waved wildly to someone in the crowd below. "Wish, Wish!" she called. She turned to Aunt Dora. "See him, Dora? See him? Right over there!" Mom pointed, but Patsy couldn't identify an uncle she hardly remembered among the bunches of people on the wharf.

Patsy was more concerned with getting off this steamer. Her anxious eyes darted about in search of the seaman who had carried her like a baby aboard the Burgeo. But there was a different one standing at the bottom of the puny steps, and he seemed like he was going to stay where he was, sucking on a cigar.

She decided to get it over with. Clutching Mom's arm with both hands, Patsy shuffled from the solid, safe deck onto the rickety piece of metal that bridged the deep gap between boat and wharf. The landing rattled and shifted under their feet. Stiff with terror, Patsy groped for the next step. Not daring to look down, she felt her way and, step by shaky step, edged down the rattley contraption. She breathed only when she'd set her feet securely on the wharf.

She stood back as Mom and Aunt Dora greeted Uncle Wish. Uncle was hardly taller than Mom or Aunt Dora. But Patsy was most surprised by his ears. They stuck out like hers! Fitzpatrick ears, Mom called them. Right away she decided she liked Uncle Wish.

A shy grin settled around his mouth and his tanned face reddened while they hugged him and then hugged him again.

"Mom is waiting," he said, pushing back his stocking cap and scratching his head like he didn't know what to do with his large hands now that the hugging was over. "You go on around. I'll get the suitcases."

"Here's Patsy," Mom said, nudging Patsy nearer her uncle.

Uncle Wish grinned at Patsy and ruffled her hair. And he kissed the pudgy hand Florence Anne reached out in an attempt to grab the stocking cap off his head. Gran must have knitted that cap. It had the same snowflake pattern Mom used in Patsy's mitts! Mom had learned it from Gran when she was a girl.

As Wish went off to find the suitcases, they edged away from the still-crowded wharf and up the hill to the road. They were no cars in Shoal Harbour. The road was nothing more than a well-beaten path worn smooth of rocks and grass except here and there in the middle.

The walk around the shore seemed to take forever. People opened front doors and came out to welcome Mom and Aunt Dora home. Florence Anne lapped up the attention and made threatening noises whenever it abated.

But Patsy was anxious to get to Gran's house. Mom told her it was the last one in the bottom of the small harbour. Maybe she could spot it. She climbed a rock twice her height. However, a blue house with a peaked roof blocked her view. Instead, she looked down on the boats below. There were lots of them. Everyone in Shoal Harbour must own a boat.

"Patsy," Mom called. "See Wish rowing across?"

Patsy shaded her eyes to look at the man standing up in the yellow dory he rowed across the harbour. The oars dipped evenly and the boat cut through the water.

"You should have gone with him," Mom said.

"What's he doing?" Patsy asked.

"He's bringing the suitcases to the house," said Mom.

"In the boat?" She couldn't believe it! Wait until Jeanette heard this.

She wondered where Uncle tied up the dory. If it was near the house, maybe she'd be allowed to sit in it. She wouldn't disturb his fishing gear.

Across the harbour the steep green hills were thick with stands of trees. Nobody lived over there. The gentler slopes on this side had grassy meadows and knobs of rocks. Patsy couldn't wait to put on her old clothes and climb them, or maybe she'd go down to the shore first. If they ever got there. She'd spent so much of this day waiting she was ready to explode.

Aunt Dora called, "Patsy, it's the white house with the red-and-black trim down there on the waterfront."

Patsy looked down where Aunt Dora pointed. She saw two houses at the end of the road, set off from the others in a wee cove where the harbour began to curve seaward. The tiny inlet, only a dip in the shoreline really, was called Fitzpatrick's Bight. Mom had talked about it hundreds of times.

Right away Patsy knew that the tan house snug to Gran's belonged to Marion, Mom's cousin. Mom had told her. Patsy also knew about Marion's girls, one a year-and-a-half older than Patsy and the other almost a year younger. She knew their names too. Loretta and Maggie. She hoped they were friendly.

Gran's house was tight to the water's edge! And attached to the front was a stage. Patsy could step out Gran's front door and stand right on the stagehead. That must be where Uncle tied up his dory. If Jeanette could only see this!

Aunt Dora took Florence Anne out of her stroller. Patsy could see why. The house was tucked under a steep grassy bank with a footpath that led down from the road. The path was so narrow it barely disturbed the rocks and tall grass.

And there was Gran in the doorway. One hand shielded her eyes from the evening sun and the other waved to them. Patsy felt shy again and waited for Mom. She watched while they hugged and cried and waited her turn to be gathered to Gran's bosom.

Gran held out her arms. "Come give your Gran a big hug," she said, smiling at Patsy through tears.

Patsy stepped into the circle of Gran's arms. She was surprised at her grandmother's strength.

"I waited a long time for this hug," Gran said, releasing her just enough to plant hearty kisses on both cheeks.

"I always wanted to come and visit you, Gran." Patsy looked into her grandmother's lively blue eyes. They were the same colour as Mom's.

"Well, your Gran is sure glad you're here, my trout."

And she hugged Patsy again.

Patsy's head reached Gran's gold wire-rimmed glasses. She hadn't thought of her grandmother as being so short.

"You'll have to tell me all about your trip," Gran said. With her arm around Patsy, she led the way inside. "Did you like the Burgeo?"

"Oh yes, Gran! It was my first time on a big steamer. I just loved it! I even got my sea legs!" Patsy told her. She left out the part about boarding the boat.

Gran chuckled and kissed her hand.

"Patsy," Mom said, taking off her coat, "put this in the front room." She gestured to a door. "Here's Aunt Dora's too."

Patsy walked through the kitchen into a hallway. Before her was a set of stairs and to the right a small room, the front room judging by the furniture. Left of the stairs, the hallway led to a lace-curtained door at the end. Curiosity swept her along the hall. She slid the curtain aside. She was right. The door did open onto the stagehead. If only Jeanette were here to go exploring with her. She laid the coats on a chair in the front room and returned to the kitchen.

She looked leisurely around at the frilly-curtained windows and the wooden chairs with their carved backs and seat cushions that matched the curtains. The rocking chair by the stove had a bright afghan laid neatly over the back and on a shelf above sat a big radio encased in dark polished wood. The table was already set for supper.

Gran reached into the wood box for a chunk of firewood and put it in the stove. Then she put the kettle on to boil.

Patsy's eyes followed her. She wondered how long the hair was that Gran had wound into a bun at the nape of her neck. There were only a few grey streaks though her grandmother was seventy-four years old. Patsy had never met her grandfather. He had died a long time ago, before she was born.

Gran sat down in the rocking chair. There was a half-knitted sock lying on the armrest.

The kitchen door opened then and two girls came in. They stood against the wall next to the door. The tall girl with chin-length straight brown hair was serious looking, but the shorter one grinned all over her small freckled face.

Gran introduced them. "This is Loretta and Maggie, Marion's girls."

"Hi," Patsy said, admiring Maggie's long, thick, coal-black plaits. Her own were so short because Mom trimmed them practically every day after she'd plaited Patsy's hair. She hated uneven ends.

"Hi," both girls spoke together.

Mom smiled affectionately at them. To Loretta she said, "The last time I saw you, you were only three!" Then she looked at Maggie. "And you were just a baby."

"Smaller than your cousin here," said Aunt Dora, sitting Florence Anne on the floor.

"Tom's working in Bishop's Falls, isn't he?" Mom said to Gran.

Gran nodded. "Marion's leaving at the end of the month so the girls can start school there in September."

"It'll be good to see Marion again. It's been a long time," Aunt Dora said. "Are you excited about moving to Bishop's Falls?" she asked the girls.

"I can't wait," Loretta said.

But Maggie shook her head so hard her long plaits jiggled. "Not me," she said. "I don't want to leave. I wish I could stay in Shoal Harbour."

"Marion drops in every day to see how I'm doing," Gran said. "I'll miss them something awful."

Surprised to hear the quaver in her grandmother's voice, Patsy looked from Mom to Aunt Dora. Neither spoke. Didn't Gran know they'd come to take her home with them?

"Why don't you go outdoors with the girls and look around a bit?" Mom said.

A grin spread across Maggie's pixie face. "We can go out in the dinghy," she said.

Patsy whirled around to face Mom. "Can we?" she squealed.

5. Gran's News

"First one down pulls 'er in."
Before Patsy realized what Loretta meant, the older girl had rounded the side of Gran's house and raced down the embankment. Her long legs easily out-ran Maggie and Patsy. They followed her down to the landwash, where Loretta picked up the mooring rope tied to a post on their stagehead.

Patsy watched every move. Hand over hand, Loretta pulled the inch-thick cable in off the water, shaking it every now and then to get rid of the seaweed that came with it. As she pulled, she wound the dripping rope around the post well above its high-water mark.

The tide had turned but was still low enough for the girls to board the dinghy from the landwash. Patsy stud-ied the slight imprint of her sneakers among the scatter of rocks and seaweed and the odd jellyfish or starfish that littered the damp, firm seabed. In a few hours the water would cover everything and be over halfway up the stages around the harbour.

Maggie yelled to an open window on the side of their house. "M-o-o-om, we're taking the dinghy out."

Patsy could see no one.

A voice from inside the house called, "Don't be long. It's almost suppertime."

"Get the oars, Mag," Loretta ordered, as she looped the rope one last time and wiped her cold, wet hands on her pants.

"Who made you the boss?" Maggie retorted, but she stalked off toward the stage. Over her shoulder she called, "You're bailing then."

Patsy noticed a second dinghy keel-up on a slip at the high tide mark. She read the upside-down print on the bow. "Bay Boy." Whose boat was that, she wondered?

"Come on," Loretta said.

Patsy traipsed after her to the dinghy bobbing on lops in less than a foot of water. Loretta pulled the boat alongside a rock that was only partly submerged by the incoming tide. The dinghy scraped bottom.

Maggie joined them, lugging the oars and a bailer. She tossed the bailer at Loretta and shoved the oars aboard. "Jump in," she told Patsy.

When Patsy hesitated, Loretta patted the dinghy's wooden frame. "Step on the rock," she said. "Then put your knee here on the gunnel and hoist yourself over the side."

Patsy took a giant step like in the game "One, Two, Three, Redlight." A small but freezing-cold wave washed over the rock and seeped in through the toes of her sneakers. She placed her knee gingerly on the spot Loretta had indicated, wobbled, and steadied herself before daring to lift her other foot. She clambered aboard and crawled crab-like to the stern.

Loretta jumped in after her and started bailing. "Does the boat leak?" Patsy asked, careful to sound casual.

"Nah." Loretta replied, rocking the dinghy to the side so she could dip the last of the water. "A drop of rainwater, that's all."

Maggie untied the boat and leapt aboard. She quat down and hauled two sets of round pegs from her pocket. "Know what these are?" she asked Patsy.

When Patsy shook her head, Maggie said, "Tholepins. They're for the oars, see?"

Patsy hadn't seen tholepins before. Jeanette's dad had metal oar-locks all in one piece.

Maggie inserted the pegs into slots in the gunnel. Then she scrambled forward and perched high on the bow.

Loretta, on the middle thwart, pushed off with an oar and pointed the bow to open harbour. Then she fitted the oars between the tholepins. "Do you know how to row?" she asked Patsy.

"Yeah," Patsy lied. "My friend Jeanette's dad took us out in his boat, and he let us row."

"After me, you can try," Maggie called back.

A short time later she hopped off the prow. "Your turn's up," she informed Loretta's back.

Patsy knew from the set of Loretta's chin that she didn't like the bossy tone of Maggie's voice. But Maggie was already standing over her, so Loretta moved to the bow. Patsy sensed that if she hadn't been there Loretta wouldn't have let her younger sister row just yet.

Maggie pulled on the oars with long even strokes. It didn't look so hard. Patsy felt confident she'd be able to do it and went back to trailing her hand in the water.

After a while Maggie pulled in the oars and crossed them

on her knees. "Come, sit here, maid," she said. She waited while Patsy crawled forward, then exchanged places.

It sounded funny to be called maid, but Patsy had no time to ask about it. She eased one oar between the tholepins and slid it into the water, holding so tightly her knuckles whitened. But then she couldn't get the other one to slide into place.

Loretta saw her problem. "Pull the oar back into the boat until you set the other one between the tholepins. Then slide them into the water together," she instructed Patsy.

Patsy did as she was told. She bit her lip in concentration and tried to lift both oars out of the water at the same time. But the oars wouldn't move the way they were supposed to. One swung high above the water, while the other trailed in the harbour. She wished she hadn't lied about being able to row.

Maggie laughed, "That's some style you got there, maid."

"Yes," agreed Loretta, with a titter. "We should enter you in the St. John's regatta."

The oar slapped the surface, startling the three girls with a shower of icy spray. The quiet harbour echoed with their squeals.

"Hey," Maggie sputtered between fits of giggles. "We're not fish. We don't need all this water."

Patsy laughed right in the middle of lifting the oars again. This time both oars slapped the water, and the girls cowered in helpless laughter as heavy spray soaked them.

Loretta lowered her arms. "Who did you say taught you how to row?" she teased. "Shove over." She sat on the thwart next to Patsy. "I'll take this oar, and you use the other one."

Patsy watched her raise the oar with both hands and lower it with the ease of an expert. She tried to do the same. The boat moved. Loretta paced her strokes with Patsy's, and they moved jerkily through the water.

From the stern Maggie giggled. "You're making me get seasick," she said, holding her stomach.

Loretta laughed. Patsy joined in, but she was determined to get it right. She tried her hardest to match her strokes to Loretta's, though her arms felt like they were being yanked from her body.

"It's time for supper," Loretta said. "You'd better let me bring her in."

Patsy watched. She'd give anything to be able to row like that. Loretta handled those oars like she was born with them in her hands.

As they tied up, Aunt Marion came down to meet them. Tall and thin, she wore pants and rubber boots and had thick black hair like Maggie's that was pulled back with an elastic band. "Don't you worry, Patsy," she said. "Within a day or two you'll be rowing as good as the girls."

Patsy's grin was sheepish. Aunt Marion must have seen her flailing the oars in the harbour.

"And make sure you let her have her turn," she ordered Maggie and Loretta, pretending to frown at them.

At the supper table, Patsy polished off a second piece of halibut. "Maggie and Loretta can row just as good as

Jeanette's dad," she said.

"Pretty soon you'll be good too," Uncle Wish told her. "All it takes is a bit of practice. You'll be a bayman in no time."

"What's a bayman?" she asked.

Uncle Wish winked at her but didn't answer.

Mom, getting up to clear the table, told her. "A bayman is someone from the bay, like us. We're from Fortune Bay. A townie's from the city and doesn't know a thing about boats."

Patsy laughed at Uncle Wish. "I'm a bayman already. I'm your niece, and you're a bayman. I just have to learn to row."

Gran patted Patsy's hand. "Tomorrow I'll have ye girls row over and mail a letter for me."

"Really?" Patsy asked, her voice squeaky with excitement. "Where?"

"Across the harbour. At the post office in Martha's shop."

"Wow!" Patsy said, intrigued by the idea of using a boat to run errands. She wished she could do it right now.

She fed Florence Anne mashed potatoes while Gran tidied up and Mom and Aunt Dora washed dishes. Aunt Dora carried hot water from the stove to the sink. There was no electricity in Shoal Harbour. The tap carried cold water, but when she needed hot Gran used the stove. A pump in the porch provided well water for drinking.

After Florence had fallen asleep on a blanket on the kitchen floor, Patsy lay down on the daybed by the window. She closed her eyes for a minute, but perked up again to watch Mom and Aunt Dora line a trunk, whose lid Uncle Wish had removed, with soft homemade quilts for the baby to sleep in. She smiled at her little cousin, asleep in her strange crib.

Yawning, she tucked her hands under her chin and watched Gran light the kerosene lamps. How cozy the soft yellow light was. Her eyes flickered like the shadows on the kitchen wall.

Some time later Patsy stirred. Not sure what had wakened her, she dismissed it and turned in to the wall. Then she heard the silence. Eyes still closed, but with her mind alert, she listened. Still no one spoke, though Patsy knew she wasn't alone. Again she heard the sound and knew for sure this time she wasn't dreaming. Heaving sobs, man-sized sobs, filled the kitchen as surely as her heavy arms ached.

Patsy stiffened. Wide-eyed with shock, she stared at the wall. Her whole body strained to know more and at the same time dreaded to hear.

Someone crossed the floor. "Wish, come back and live with us, you and Mom," Aunt Dora said.

Uncle Wish blew his nose loud and hard. Then he said, "I don't know what to do, Dora. All I know is fishin. I fished here all me life. I don't know what to do."

Patsy turned to face the room. No one noticed.

She tried not to look at Uncle, but the more she tried not to the more she couldn't stop herself. Uncle stared at his vamps. Patsy tried not to gawk at the shiny wet spot on his cheek.

Gran stopped knitting in mid-row. She laid the sock on her lap and rubbed her fingers vigorously.

Patsy had heard Gran tell Mom that sometimes her knuckles swelled with arthritis and ached so badly that she couldn't hold the needle. But if Gran's arthritis was acting up, she wouldn't rub her sore fingers that hard.

Gran was sore all right. But it wasn't her joints. Patsy could see the rigid set of her face. Gran was so worked up her hands shook. She rubbed them to control her agitation. When she spoke, her voice shook too. "Well, Aloysius," she said, "I know what we're goin to do. We're stayin right here." Her voice grew stronger with determination. "We're not movin, and that's that." She punctuated her words with a determined nod of her head.

Patsy knew she meant every word.

There was a long, troubled silence.

Aunt Dora's voice didn't sound so certain. "But Mom," she said finally, "there'll be nothing here. They'll cut off the mail, the coastal boat…everything."

Gran folded her arms and leaned back in the rocking chair. She said nothing.

Mom rubbed her hand in circles on the embroidered tablecloth. "It's an awful thing they're doing to people," she said, a quaver in her voice. "What in the name of God are they thinking about?" To Uncle Wish she said, "What did they say in the meetings?"

Uncle Wish sighed and stood up. He went to the stove and poured himself some tea before he answered. "They said it costs too much to service the outports. They'll help pay for the move."

Mom shook her head. "When will they stop the coastal service?" she asked.

"Next June," Uncle Wish replied.

In a voice as controlled as the tension on her knitting needles, Gran said, "Anything can happen over the winter…anything." She picked up her knitting.

For sure Gran and Uncle Wish wouldn't be coming home with them. Patsy shut her eyes tight and squeezed back tears. When Mom noticed Patsy was awake and asked if she wanted a mug-up before bed, she shook her head.

"It's time to say goodnight then," Mom said.

Patsy's shoulders slumped under the heaviness in the room. She leaned over Gran's chair and kissed her grandmother's flushed cheek. Gran returned the kiss. Though Patsy felt shyer still after having heard Uncle cry, she hugged him hard. She could smell the sea on his plaid work shirt.

"Goodnight, little bayman," Uncle said. He ruffled her hair.

Mom took a lamp from the sideboard to light the way up the narrow stairs.

Patsy was intrigued. "Can I hold it? I'll be careful," she pleaded.

Mom, looking too worn to hold out, passed Patsy the lamp. She hovered close, and Patsy led the way to their small, snug bedroom.

Once in the room she said, "Gran and Uncle Wish aren't coming home with us, are they?"

As if she hadn't heard Patsy, Mom opened their suitcase and took out Patsy's pyjamas.

Patsy lay under homemade quilts watching the flickering shadows the lamp made on the flowery wallpaper. "Look, Mom, on the wall, look," she said.

Mom struggled with a stuck drawer. She nodded absently. But Patsy knew she wasn't seeing the shadows, not these shadows anyway.

6. A Harbour Dip

Patsy sat at the table next to Aunt Dora as she fed Florence Anne. Her aunt pried loose a piece of toast squeezed tight in the baby's fist. Patsy grinned and kissed the one clean spot she could find on her little cousin's cheek.

"Where's Uncle Wish?" she asked Aunt Dora.

Gran answered. "He's not back from fishing yet." She glanced at the clock on the stove. "Won't be long now before he'll be in for a cup of tea."

"Do you want some more toast, Patsy?" Mom asked.

Another morning Patsy would have taken a second slice of Gran's toasted homemade bread and blueberry jam, but she had no time to waste on eating this morning.

Last evening Gran had said Patsy and the girls could row across the harbour to mail her letters.

Patsy was eager to be underway. She eyed the envelopes on the corner of the radio shelf. "Can we go mail the letters now?" she asked, putting her plate in the sink.

"Just leave your dishes, dear," Aunt Dora said. "I'll

do them after I feed the baby."

Mom caught Gran's eye and said, "I wish she was this anxious to run errands at home."

Gran teased, "I guess you'll just have to get a boat, Mae."

"If you and Uncle Wish come live with us, we'll have a boat," Patsy blurted. Before the words were out, she knew she'd said the wrong thing.

Gran pursed her lips and, turning her back to the room, wiped the kettle with the dishcloth she held.

Mom gave Patsy a look that warned her not to say anything more. Patsy hated that look. It made her feel like she'd done something dreadful.

Gran reached up to the radio shelf for her letters and handed them to Patsy. "Be careful now. Make sure you don't fool around in the boat."

"I'll be careful," Patsy said. "Do you need anything at the shop, Gran? I can get it. I have money."

"Oh, you do, eh? Well now, I'm partial to peppermint knobs. Martha has some lovely ones."

Patsy grinned at Gran. "Okay, I'll bring you back some," she promised, happy to be able to make up for her thoughtless words.

She half skipped, half ran, round the side of the house and spotted the girls and Aunt Marion by the white dinghy still keel-up on the slip. This morning the high tide lapped at its very edge. Patsy waved the letters and called to Maggie and Loretta, "We have to go mail these for Gran."

"Come help us," Maggie grunted from the side of the dinghy.

"What are you doing?" Patsy asked.

Loretta stood at the bow and Aunt Marion, wearing work gloves that were way too big, was at the stern.

"Mom said we could take out Mike's dinghy," Loretta informed her. "Maggie whined and nagged all last night."

Maggie replied by sticking out her tongue at her sister.

With her feet planted apart, Aunt Marion barked orders. She looked like she could right that dingy all by herself if she'd a mind to. At the count of three, they turned the "Bay Boy" over and slid it off the slip into the water. High tide, and Aunt Marion, sure made light work.

"You better take good care of it," said the girls' mother. She held the painter while Loretta put the oars aboard. "If you so much as scratch the paint, Mike will be as sore as a hooked sculpin." A bit of a grin snuck around the corners of her mouth. Her eye caught Patsy's slightly anxious look and she winked.

"Mike's our brother. He works in Bishop's Falls with Dad," Maggie told Patsy as they climbed in.

"Grandfather Farrel built the dinghy for Mike the year before he died," Loretta added. "Didn't he, Mom?"

"That's right," said their mother. "Mike was his only grandson and Grandfather spoiled him rotten." She tossed the painter aboard.

The dinghy was a perfect size. Patsy felt sure she'd be able to row this one with no problems. It too was flat-bottomed, which made it steady, but it was narrower than the one they'd used yesterday and not quite so long. She imagined herself at the oars.

Maggie rowed across the harbour. In no time at all

the girls were tying up at a stage below the post office. Patsy tucked the letters into the pocket of her shorts so she could use both hands to climb.

She picked her way across the scraggy, uneven scrub spruce of the stagehead. Trees never grew well on the rocky coast of Newfoundland. The biggest one under-foot was hardly thicker than her arm. The different sizes nailed end-to-end left gaps that didn't seem to hinder Loretta and Maggie at all. They skipped across and waited for Patsy before climbing the bank to the shop above.

Miss Martha, as the girls called the friendly old woman who served them, took the letters at the post office wicket and then shuffled around the corner to the shop counter.

Miss Martha already knew who Patsy was and told her she must look like her dad since she didn't seem to have her mother's features. "But you have your mother's love of the water, I hear. When Mae was a girl, she fair lived in the boats. She even went fishing with the boys when they'd let her," Miss Martha told Patsy, a distant look in her eyes. "And now, 'tis almost all gone." She sighed. "What can I get you, my dear?"

Patsy bought Gran's peppermint knobs and some chocolate to share. She looked around the tiny shop while Maggie and Loretta chose their treats and chat-ted with Miss Martha.

The shop was hardly bigger than Patsy's bedroom at home. It was crowded with only the three of them. A barrel of salt beef sat by the door. The tidy shelves were packed tight with everything from canned food, bolts of cloth, brooms, and rubber boots, to Christmas decorations tucked away in the far corner of the top shelf. Patsy was amazed at the quantity of goods in one small room.

She poked Gran's candy in one pocket of her shorts and her own in another until she was aboard the dinghy again.

Loretta took the oars. Once they were away from the stage, she pulled them in and crossed them on the bottom of the dinghy. Then she secured them with her feet. The paddle ends rested on the gunnel while the girls ate their candy.

Patsy asked, "What are you going to do with the boats when you leave?"

Maggie shrugged. "Take them with us." As far as she was concerned that was the only thing to do.

"Are you crazy, Mag?" Loretta cut in. "We're never gonna be able to take the boats. We'll probably have to sell them."

"You're the one who's crazy, Loret," Maggie deliberately left off the last part of her sister's name. "Mom would never sell the boats, especially not Mike's." She stood and leaned toward her sister. Her face was pale and tight.

"That's what you think," Loretta shot back. "I heard Mom tell Gran she might."

"You're lying, Loretta." Maggie's voice cracked.

"Am not. Ask her," retorted her sister, blowing a bubble with her gum.

Patsy knew from Maggie's face that the argument wasn't over. Crying, Maggie yelled at Loretta. "You don't care anyway." Supporting herself with her arms, she reached out and kicked her sister hard on the ankle.

Loretta yelped and kicked back. The "Bay Boy," steady though it was, rocked with the sudden movement.

Petrified, Patsy gripped the stern. She gaped in stunned silence as an oar slipped through the tholepins and overboard.

"Now look what you did!" Loretta barked at Maggie. She grabbed for the oar, but it had drifted beyond reach.

They were well out in the harbour. In Patsy's mind they might as well have been adrift in open sea. "Jump off after it," she squawked, in a tizzy.

"We can't swim," Loretta said.

Maggie was bawling.

The oar drifted farther.

In one motion Patsy kicked off her sneakers, emptied her pockets, and plunged into the harbour. The shocking cold pressed close. She lost her breath and her nerve.

Dimly aware of the girls' screaming, she gasped for air and tried to stand like she could in the swimming hole back home. Her toes stretched down into numbing cold. Her head submerged, and she gulped a mouthful of salty water. She clawed her way to the surface, retched, and spat out the vile taste.

Patsy's only thought was the oar which seemed to be gathering speed on waves that hadn't been there before. Then she realized it was she churning the water. In her panic she'd forgotten all she'd learned in swimming lessons. Thrashing desperately after the oar, she was actually going nowhere. And she was tiring fast.

Salty water dribbled down her bangs and into her

eyes. Everything around her was a blur. She licked her lips and tasted salt. She could even smell it. Her sodden clothes stuck to her skin and dragged her down to colder depths.

The scream of her name buoyed her. Squint-eyed, she spotted the oar bobbing on lops about four or five boat lengths away.

Dipping her face in the water, she swam as fast and as long as she could. She lifted her head to take a breath and a sighting on the oar. There it was just a half dozen strokes away....

Her right hand closed around the cold, wet wood. She tried to swim with the oar in her hand but splashed herself in the face. She trod water while she wiped her mouth and eyes.

Next she tried pushing it ahead of her. She could barely lift her tired, cold-deadened arm out of the water. She turned on her back to rest. Her leaden feet and arms sank. Only her face breached the surface.

Dimly Patsy heard the girls scream her name. Then a deep, slow rumble resounded off the hills and across the water. The Burgeo. She rolled over with a start.

Eyeing the dinghy, she realized she was about two boat lengths away. The girls screamed and waved with an urgency that terrified Patsy. She gave the oar a hefty shove. Then another one.

Loretta fished the oar out of the water. Maggie kept up the frantic gesturing.

Almost there. One more stroke. And then one more. Finally, Patsy clung to the dinghy like a periwinkle tight to a piling.

Maggie and Loretta grabbed her under the armpits

and hauled her in. She was numb inside and out.

Again the blow – full and deep, a rumbling burp from the Burgeo's belly.

Patsy sat bolt upright. Jeepers. The steamer, blaring its departure, loomed in mid-harbour. And the "Bay Boy" was pitched practically in her shadow.

Patsy's flushed face paled.

Maggie and Loretta looked stricken. With a shudder, Loretta grabbed the oars. "We'd better get out of here," she cried.

"Wait!" Maggie pointed to Uncle's dory. "Uncle Wish is coming!"

Around the harbour, boats of all kinds putt-putted toward them with Uncle Wish in the lead. He cut the motor as he came alongside. His face was the picture of worry. When he saw that they were okay, he waved at the other boats. Some turned back to shore. Others waited at a distance.

The Burgeo steamed out to sea.

"What did ye do?" Uncle asked, so worked up he didn't know who to look at first. His anxious eyes darted from one to the other and lingered on Patsy, soaked to the skin and looking like she'd frozen onto the middle thwart.

The girls had nothing to say. And Uncle looked too rattled to listen anyway. "Here, I'll tow ye in," he said.

Maggie settled close to Patsy and flung a protective arm around her shoulder.

Uncle fastened the dinghy's painter to the stern of the dory.

Another time the girls would have delighted in being towed in the wake of the dory's waves. But right now no one had heart for it. Patsy was all shivers. The girls were all shame.

The guilt was too much for Maggie. "It's my fault," she blubbered. "I'm some sorry, Patsy."

Patsy wiped her runny nose with the back of her hand. "Aw, das all right, maid," she said, patting Maggie's skinny knee. In her shivery voice, she imitated an old skipper. "I likes me mornin' dip, I does!"

Maggie giggled in spite of herself, and Patsy thought she saw a ghost of a grin, just for a second, on Loretta's responsible face.

Boats all around headed back too, and people who had gathered around the shore to watch and worry went about their business again.

Patsy was sorry about everything. She figured she'd be in for it when, on her first morning in Shoal Harbour, she showed up on Gran's doorstep looking like a drowned rat. A drowned harbour rat. Especially after Gran said not to fool around in the boat.

She bit her lip. She'd just had the most awful thought. What if Aunt Marion took away the dinghy?

Patsy might never have a turn rowing the "Bay Boy."

7. *Talk About Moving*

Patsy sloshed across the stagehead. She didn't want to be in trouble at Gran's place. Right now she'd rather eat the grizzle parts of a dozen cod tongues than face everybody.

She dragged her waterlogged body around the corner of the house. Uncle Wish was quick behind her. He caught up to Patsy in the porch and laid his hand on her sodden shoulder. "Your mom and Dora went visiting a while ago," he said.

She nodded. Between shivers of cold and nerves, her mouth wasn't under her control yet. Biting her lower lip did nothing to stop the trembling.

Uncle Wish opened the door. Gran stopped sweeping the floor. "Good heavens...."

Uncle Wish cut in. "Patsy showed us how she can swim. In fact, she showed the whole harbour." He grinned at her.

Poor Gran looked puzzled.

"She'll tell us about it after she dries off," he said to Gran.

Gran ignored the pool forming on the floor. She ushered Patsy into the bathroom where she pulled three thick towels from the back of the cupboard.

"Wrap one around your head," she said, and spread another on the floor for Patsy to stand on. "Now get out of those wet things. I'll bring you some warm water."

Gran bustled off to the kitchen and returned in no time with water from the big, grey kettle that simmered all day long on the back of the wood stove. She fussed a bit more and hovered outside the bathroom door while Patsy washed off the salt and changed into dry clothes.

After, Patsy curled up in the rocking chair by the stove. Gran toweled her hair. "Now tell us how you came to be out in the middle of the harbour."

Patsy clapped her hand to her mouth. "Oh Gran," she said, "I left your peppermint knobs in the boat."

"Never mind the candy." Exasperated, Gran rubbed faster. "You can get them later. Tell us what happened."

Uncle Wish leaned forward on the straight-backed chair, elbows on his knees. One hand rubbed his chin. Patsy caught his eye. She was sure he was hiding a grin, but didn't know if it was because of Gran, or herself. She began her story.

Gran nodded impatiently at the parts about mailing the letters and buying candy and listened with care to Patsy's recounting of the argument between Maggie and Loretta.

Patsy caught the terse shake of Gran's head. She

continued. "Maggie got really mad when Loretta said their mom was going to sell the boats. She kicked Loretta and Loretta kicked her back, and the oar fell overboard. I jumped off after it."

Gran laid the damp towel on the chair back. "Bloody government," she said, planting her hands on her hips. "The whole harbour is in an uproar, even the children."

Uncle Wish leaned back and reached in his pocket for tobacco and papers. He rolled a cigarette. Then he stared at his grey vamps and didn't light it.

Gran ladled up a bowl of chicken soup. "Come and get this inside you," she ordered Patsy. "It'll warm your bones."

Patsy sat at the table. She looked up at Gran. "Do you think Mom'll be very mad when she finds out?" she asked.

"I dare say she knows by now." Uncle Wish chuckled. "Half the harbour was out in the boats and the other half watching from the shore. I'd say the news might have hit Beachy Cove right about now." He tweaked her nose. Then he buttered himself a slice of bread.

Gran moved the crackers closer to Patsy. "Don't you worry about your mom," she said. "Mae was in plenty of scrapes herself out in the boats."

Patsy finished the soup and moved back to the comfort of Gran's chair. Gran covered her legs with the afghan. Her eyes were closing when Mom arrived in a bluster with Aunt Dora and the baby close behind.

Mom was worked up all right. She swooped down

on Patsy with a hundred questions all trying to get out of her at once.

Gran fended her off. "Now, Mae, it's all over. You can see she's fine."

Patsy went through the whole story again. With every breath Mom was feeling her forehead and asking, "How are you feeling? Are you chilly? Are you sure you're okay?"

Patsy shook her head each time. After, she tried to rest like Mom said, but Loretta and Maggie's argument stuck in her mind. If Aunt Marion had to sell stuff, would Gran and Uncle Wish have to do the same? Would they have to sell Uncle Wish's boat? And what about the house and all of Gran's things?

Restless, Patsy wandered from window to window. She told Mom she was going up on the hill behind Gran's house. "I won't stay long," she promised.

Patsy climbed the path to the road. She smiled to herself. She certainly didn't need to check for cars before crossing. From habit, though, she looked left and right. She was surprised to see two men walking up the road toward her.

The one in the brown suit who caught Patsy's eye first was doing all the talking. Good and loud too. He flourished one hand as he talked, while he gripped a black satchel in the other. There didn't look to be much in it. The other fellow looked ordinary and dressed ordinary in rubber boots and work pants. A navy stocking cap was pushed back on his red head. He said nothing. At least not a word since Patsy had spotted them.

The suit man stopped in his tracks and looked down

on the Bight. He gestured toward Gran and Aunt Marion's houses. "Now who would that be living there?" The breeze lifted his coattail and Patsy saw his belly spilling over his belt.

The other fellow replied. A quieter sort he was, but Patsy could still hear. "Now right there below, that's Tom Farrel's place. He already signed. Moving at the end of the month, I hear."

The suit man nodded. "And there?" He looked down on Gran's house.

The other fellow hesitated. "That's Wish Fitzpatrick's place. He lives there with his mother."

The suit man boomed, "Should we pay a visit, do you think?"

With a fierce shake of his head, the other fellow said, "No sir, I don't think that would be such a good idea."

The suit man turned on his muddy heel. "Drop in to see them. Tell them...."

"No sir, I'll not be dropping in. They know everything they need to know."

Patsy watched them walk back the way they'd come. She didn't like the suit man. Too bad he wouldn't twist his ankle on a loose rock.

She climbed as high as she could without breaking her promise to Mom. She sat on a rocky outcrop and watched the two men until they disappeared into a house farther up the harbour. They must be from the government, at least the suit man must be. She wouldn't say a word to Gran. Not one iota.

Her eyes traveled to the area of the harbour where she'd jumped overboard. She giggled, warm and safe in the midday sun, and wondered if she'd been the first to ever swim in the deep harbour. She'd have to ask Maggie and Loretta why they couldn't swim.

Her chance came shortly. She looked down to see Loretta open the door and let it slam shut behind her.

Loretta spotted Patsy, waved, and climbed to join her.

"Where's Maggie?" Patsy asked. This was the first time she'd seen one sister without the other.

Loretta plopped down on a rock. "Aw, she's still bawling about the boat."

"What about it?" Patsy asked, dreading Loretta's reply. "Can't we go out in it any more?"

"Not today," Loretta told her. "Mom said if you weren't here she'd haul it out of the water for good. But that's not why Mag's crying. She's carrying on about Mom selling the dinghies."

"Oh," Patsy said, breathing easier. She was immediately ashamed of her selfishness. She had no business thinking of herself when Maggie was in a fit over losing the boats. "Is your mom really going to sell them?" she asked.

"I don't know," Loretta replied. "I wish Dad would come back and we'd move and get it over with."

"You don't mind going, do you?" Patsy asked.

"In a way I do," Loretta said. "I'll miss everybody and all that. But I'm excited to go to a new school and meet girls my own age instead of hanging around with Mag all the time. And Dad just bought a new car. We haven't seen it yet." She pulled on a blade of stubborn grass, laid it between her thumbs, and brought it to her mouth and whistled.

"How come you and Maggie can't swim?" Patsy asked.

Loretta let the light breeze blow the blade away. "I

dunno," she replied. "No one tried to teach us. We spend most of our time in the boats. Sometimes we go to Collins' Cove when it's really hot. But the water's still pretty cold."

"Where's Collins' Cove?" Patsy wanted to know.

Loretta swivelled around. "Just up over the hill."

Patsy looked.

"See that path up there? If you follow it for ten minutes or so, it'll take you to Collins' Cove."

"Can we go?" Patsy squeaked excitedly.

Below, a door slammed. Maggie emerged. She kicked at some rocks, picked one up, and threw it half-heartedly into the water.

"Let's call out to her," she said to Loretta.

Together they yelled Maggie's name. She turned at the sound and climbed up to them. There was certainly no spring to her steps.

When she reached them, Patsy saw that her eyes were still red from crying.

She squeezed onto the rock with Patsy. In her forthright manner she said, "Mom said she has to sell Dad's dinghy, but she promised to keep the 'Bay Boy.'"

"Yeah," said her sister, "but she doesn't know yet when, or how, we'll get it to Bishop's Falls."

"At least you get to keep it," Patsy said.

"Yup." Maggie pushed her black bangs off her forehead. "But we have to leave in just three more weeks." The tone of her voice was fierce. "When I'm grown up and have lots of money, I'm coming back here. And no government will tell me what to do."

Loretta leaned across Patsy to look at her sister. "Get outa here, Mag. You'll never come back here to live.

You'll get used to town life, and you'll like it."

Maggie's eyes blazed. "Loretta Farrel, if you don't want to be knocked off that rock, you better shut up."

Patsy was glad she was sitting between them. She knew Maggie would really do it.

To distract the girls, she said, "Did you see those two fellows going around the harbour? One had a suit on."

Maggie snorted. "That's Syl Pardy from Beachy Cove with the government fella. The government hired Syl to go around with their man to keep him from getting lynched."

"Go away, Mag, that's not true," Loretta retorted.

"Not one word of it is a lie," insisted Maggie. "Cross my heart and hope to die." To prove she was telling the truth she made the sign of the cross over her heart. "I heard Skipper Phonse and old Uncle Wally Davage having a yarn with Mr. Joe-Mike down on the wharf. They were laughing at Syl Pardy. Government Pardy they called him. They said it was a good name for Syl because he's so thick with them anyway."

Patsy sensed another argument brewing. "Hey," she said brightly, "why don't we go to Collins' Cove tomorrow, and I'll teach you how to swim?"

The black look left Maggie's face and a lilt returned to her voice. "Really, maid?" she said, bounding to her feet. "Collins' Cove is one of my most favorite places! You'll just love it, Patsy! I hope it's nice and hot tomorrow, eh, Loretta?"

8. Collins' Cove

Patsy and Maggie sat on rocks by the side of the road waiting for Loretta. Towels hung around their necks and two paper bags on the ground beside them held drinks, sandwiches, and chips.

Maggie called down the hill. "Loretta, why are you bringing that big blanket?"

Loretta strode toward them. She tucked the grey blanket under her arm. "I hate getting sand all over me."

"Then lie on your towel." Maggie sounded like she was telling something very simple to a small child.

Patsy hoped there wouldn't be an argument before they got underway, but Loretta ignored her sister and walked past them to the footpath. Without looking back to see if they were following, she began the climb.

The path looked to Patsy like a ball of dirt-brown yarn had rolled downhill, unwinding as it twisted around scraggy spruce and through sunny clearings of dandelions. It wound past a patch of purple irises by the brook until it used itself up just a few feet from the clump of cracker berry bushes growing at the edge of the road.

Maggie grabbed her bag off the ground and passed her sister to take the lead. They tramped single file over the first hill and then up the next slightly higher one. Maggie stopped only long enough to tie her sneaker.

The short break gave Patsy a chance to pull off the shirt she wore over her bathing suit and stuff it into her bag. Feeling cooler, she hurried to catch up before Loretta's long strides left her behind.

She couldn't resist stopping to pick a pretty blue harebell. She tucked it under the strap of her swimsuit and scrambled to join Maggie and Loretta at the top of the rise.

Maggie guzzled a long drink of strawberry freshie and passed the bottle to Loretta, whose swig was more civilized. She held the bottle out to Patsy and waited, lid in hand. But Patsy was busy drinking in the sight before her. She barely sipped the freshie before passing it back.

A summer meadow unscarred by rock or road stretched all the way down to the sea. And it was chock-full of wildflowers from one side to the other. Patsy picked her way through heaps of purple bachelor buttons. Farther down sturdy blue lupines waved among the long grass. And the whole meadow was caught picture-perfect between a blue sky and sea that matched exactly the delicate forget-me-nots at Patsy's feet.

She flung her arms wide. Her lungs and her senses

soaked up the potent mix of tangy sea air and wild-flower perfume. It left her lightheaded, lighthearted.

Maggie tapped her arm and raced past. "You're it," she called over her shoulder. Her black plaits flew out behind her.

Patsy took up the chase among buttercups and daisies, the tallest she'd ever seen. "Gotcha." She tagged Maggie's shoulder and they plopped down laughing near a fringe of wild rose bushes crammed with pink blooms.

"Come on, or by the time we get there it'll be time to head home again," Loretta said.

"Okay, maid," Maggie agreed. She rolled down the slope with Patsy close behind, the colours fusing in their laughing, dizzy heads.

Loretta followed. She picked up a towel here, a bag there, and slapped at the grass that tickled and scratched her legs.

The meadow came to a gentle end at a flat grassy bank. It dropped away to a curve of sandy beach beyond which lay a strip of damp, rippled strand.

Patsy dropped her towel and bag on the fine warm sand. Her feet pounded the hard-packed strand as she ran straight for the water. She gasped at the first cold splash and hopped up and down, squealing.

When she got used to it, she waded out till the water was up to her waist. The smooth rounded rocks underfoot were hard to walk on. She beckoned to Maggie. "Come on out. I'll teach you to swim."

Maggie couldn't resist. After some squeals of her own, she was soon floating on her back. She then graduated to dog paddle. She stood in water up to her thighs and swam frantically toward shore, until she scraped her toes on the bottom. Her kick displaced more water than a ship's propeller. Patsy didn't have the heart to correct her.

Loretta watched from her blanket. In her own good time she joined them, but not farther out than her knees. She refused to touch more than the tip of her nose to the water and wouldn't hear of lying down in it at all. And she squawked loud enough to be heard back in Shoal Harbour when Maggie, fed up with her, splashed her bathing suit.

Patsy showed off for them — all the skills she'd learned in swimming lessons and that she'd forgotten in her harbour dip! At last, with goose bumps as big as turnips erupting on her arms and legs, she left the water. She licked her blue salty lips to control their shivering.

Maggie and Loretta laughed at the face she made. "I thought by now you'd like the taste of salt water," Loretta teased.

After they'd devoured the sandwiches and chips and finished off the freshie, Maggie suggested, "Let's pick some foxgloves."

"Okay." Patsy was game, though she didn't know what foxgloves were.

Loretta refused. "I don't want to get stung by a bee," she said.

"You won't get stung," Maggie scoffed. "Just shake them before you pick them."

Patsy followed her to the far edge of the bank. The foxgloves were as tall as the lupines in the meadow. Maggie shook one and picked it. She then plucked off the violet blooms that grew along the stem and slipped one over each finger. Patsy did the same. They waved their hands about and pretended to be grand ladies.

Maggie giggled. "Let's take some back to Loretta."

"She'll be mad," Patsy cautioned.

Maggie flashed a wicked grin and nodded. She hurriedly picked a handful of flowers and hid them behind her back as she tiptoed back to the beach.

Patsy followed. She clamped one hand over her mouth to stifle her giggles.

"Here, Loretta, some bumblebees to visit you." Maggie dropped the bunch on Loretta's head.

Loretta grabbed for her sister's leg and missed. Then she screeched in terror as two bumblebees buzzed around her. She scrabbled to her feet, grabbed her blanket, and wrapped it about her head as she took off down the beach. When she was certain the bumblebees were gone, she charged after Maggie and chased her back and forth across the sand.

Maggie was laughing too much to run anymore. She waded into the water to catch her breath. "I'm sorry, Loretta," she apologized.

Loretta threw the foxgloves at her. "I'll let you come out if we go to the cemetery," she said, standing arms crossed with the blanket draped over her shoulders.

Maggie agreed. "We'll show you your grandfather's grave, Patsy," she said.

"Where is it?" Patsy asked. She'd seen no sign of a cemetery anywhere today.

"Around the other side of the cove," Maggie said as she trotted ahead of them across the strand.

They rounded the headland and saw a tiny cemetery

behind a white picket fence. Maggie opened the gate and walked inside. The grass was mown. The only wildflower was white yarrow growing along the fence and filling the air with a too-sweet scent.

Yarrow grew in the cemetery back home too. Patsy smelled it when she and Mom visited her father's grave. She couldn't remember anything about her dad, but she knew him through Mom's stories.

Loretta stopped by a white cross that, except for the black hand-painted name, looked like all the others. "Here's your grandfather's grave, right here." The girls made the sign of the cross. Patsy did the same. She felt strange whispering a prayer for this grandfather she had never known. She'd ask Mom to tell her about him. It was easier to pray for someone she knew.

Loretta crossed herself again. She said to Patsy, "Gran told Mom she wants to be buried next to your Grandfather Fitzpatrick. If she has to move, she'll never be able to visit his grave again."

"And she'll be buried with strangers," Maggie added.

"Well, she can be brought back here to be buried," Patsy said. Her voice was sharp with irritation.

Loretta shook her head. "Not likely," she said. "And here's Grandfather Farrel's grave." She straightened the white cross marking the grave site.

But Patsy had had enough of the cemetery and their conversation. She didn't like this place and she didn't like to think of Gran dying. She sat outside the fence pulling handfuls of grass and watching the breeze blow them away. She didn't know what Maggie and Loretta were so worried about anyway. It was none of their business. Gran wasn't their grandmother, even if they did call her Gran.

Maggie clicked the gate shut behind her. "We're coming back next week with Mom to paint the crosses before we leave," she said.

"Why? Pretty soon no one will be here to visit the graves anyway." Patsy was still mad. She wanted to make Maggie and Loretta mad too.

"If you had relatives buried here like we do, you wouldn't say that." Maggie looked her straight in the eye.

Patsy looked away feeling mean and even madder at Maggie for making her feel that way. "I do have relatives buried here," she said.

"Nobody you know," Maggie said.

Patsy couldn't argue. But she wasn't about to give in. "Anyway," she lied. "Gran is coming to live with us. Uncle Wish too."

Maggie and Loretta looked at each other and then at her. "Did Gran tell you that?" Loretta asked.

Patsy flicked her plaits. The girls stared at her. She faced them both without blinking once. Her throat was dry. "No," she said. She stuck out her chin. "No, but that's why we came, to bring her and Uncle Wish home with us."

The friendliness in Maggie's voice was gone. "Don't you think Gran should decide that for herself?" she said. She turned on her heel and tramped back the way they'd come.

Loretta shrugged and followed. Patsy let them go. But when Loretta disappeared around the cove, she hustled to keep them in sight. She didn't want to be left here.

Maggie made straight for the path with Loretta close

behind. Patsy followed at a distance. Their little parade was as solemn as a funeral procession.

Patsy stumbled on one of the zillion roots and rocks sticking out of the ground in her path. She spat out a word Mom wouldn't allow her to use and shielded her eyes from the sun as she called out to Loretta. "How much farther?"

"Almost there." Loretta, glad that someone was talking, waited for Patsy. "Just over the hill."

Patsy licked her dry lips and pushed back the bangs plastered to her forehead. The sun burned into her scorched face. Now that the breeze had died, fat bluebottles droned in their faces while mean little blackflies drew blood again and again.

Patsy trudged on close at Loretta's heels. Her head hurt like a too-tight headband digging into her scalp, and Maggie's words pounded in her ears. She was sure Maggie was leading them home by a longer route just to be miserable. Patsy couldn't remember all those rocks and roots, though Loretta assured her it was the same path.

Loretta stopped. "There's the lucky bush," she said. "Throw a rock in and make a wish." She aimed hers right for the middle of a pile of small rocks a little ways off the path. "I wish for codshead stew for supper and ice cream from Miss Martha's shop. Your turn," she said.

Patsy slumped to her knees to pick up a rock.

"Watch it!" Loretta cautioned. She pointed to a big toadstool Patsy had almost knelt on. "Fairy cap. Break it, and the fairies will take you!"

Patsy edged away from it. She threw her rock on the pile. "I wish for fishcakes and jelly." Then she added,

"And a barrel of freshie to drink." Mom never let her have freshie at mealtimes, so she'd have to be lucky.

They pushed on to the crest of the hill. There was no sign of Maggie. Maybe she'd stepped on a toadstool and the fairies had taken her. Patsy liked the idea. She tramped on behind Loretta. The lucky bush stayed in her thoughts. She should have thrown a second rock and wished for Gran to change her mind. She'd love to see the look on Maggie's face then.

Under her breath, Patsy mimicked Maggie. "Don't you think Gran should decide that for herself?" She stomped to the road, ignoring Loretta's good-bye.

The porch door was hooked back and the kitchen door held open with a shoe. Patsy kicked off her sneakers and dropped her towel on the washer in the corner of the porch.

Aunt Dora, with Florence Anne practically bobbing out of her arms, turned at the sound. "Well, you're back," she said. "We were just about to send out a search party."

Her silly words and affectionate tone couldn't coax a smile from Patsy. She brushed past Aunt Dora and the baby and collapsed on a chair. "Mom, can I have a drink?"

"Sure, my darling." Mom set down a bowl of steaming potatoes. "Tired, are you? That's a long walk to Collins' Cove." Her face was all concern. She pumped Patsy a glass of cold water.

Patsy closed her eyes to hold back the tears that tried to squeeze through her eyelids.

"Why the grum look?" Gran asked. "Did anything happen?"

Patsy shook her head.

"Are the girls home too?"

She nodded and opened her eyes long enough to take the glass from Mom.

"I think you got a sunburn today," Mom said. "Maybe you should lie down."

Patsy slumped lower. The effort to blink back the tears was too much. They slid down her cheeks.

Mom's hand on her back propelled her upstairs. "You can have some herring later if you feel like it."

Herring. Patsy hated herring. All those bones. It was just as well she hadn't made a wish about Gran at the lucky bush. It probably wouldn't come true either.

"I'm not going to sleep. I'll just lie down for a bit," she said, stubborn to the end.

As Mom was leaving the room, Patsy opened her eyes. "Leave the door open," she said. She sat up. "Maggie and Loretta showed me Grandpa's grave."

Mom looked back at her. "Wish is going to take me and Dora over in the boat. Do you want to come?"

Patsy shook her head. She lay back on the pillow and turned her head to the wall.

9. Gran's Attic

Patsy whipped the light blanket off her legs and swung her feet to the floor. A glance at the clock on the dresser told her it was seven o'clock. She was not pleased, not pleased at all. She'd slept like a baby, and they'd all let her.

Her hand slid along the railing as she marched downstairs. From the hall she saw Mom drape a sweater over her shoulders. Patsy quickened her steps. "Where're you going, Mom?"

Mom smiled. "That was some sleep you had!" She planted a kiss on Patsy's forehead and gushed, "Are you feeling better, love? Is your headache gone?"

Patsy ignored her. "Where're you going?" Aunt Dora carried a sweater too. "I'm coming," Patsy said.

Gran coaxed Patsy from her rocking chair. "You stay home with me, my trout. You can help me make some blueberry pudding for tomorrow."

But Patsy clutched at Mom's arm. "Where're you going? Why can't I go?"

"We're just going for a walk. You stay home with Gran. You need a rest this evening."

Mom wasn't giving in. Patsy folded her arms and stuck out her lip in a pout.

Gran licked the piece of yarn at the toe of the sock she was knitting before threading it through her needle. "Patsy, there's something I want to show you after you have a bite to eat," she said.

Aunt Dora was already at the door. Mom bent to kiss Patsy's cheek. Patsy turned her head. Mom wasn't getting off that easy.

The door closed and, except for the sleeping baby, Patsy was alone with Gran. The house was quiet but for the click-click of Gran's knitting needles. Patsy moped around the kitchen. She wondered what Loretta was doing. She didn't care about Maggie.

"Would you pass me those scissors on the window sill, dear?"

As Patsy picked up the scissors, she saw someone. Two someones. And she knew who they were. Fear squeezed her insides so she couldn't breathe.

Patsy watched, scissors in hand. Picking their way cautiously down the path to Gran's house were the suit man, the government man Maggie had called him, and the other fellow. Patsy's breath was as laboured as if she were sucking air through a collapsed straw.

Gran waited, hand outstretched.

"Gran," Patsy said, "there's two fellows coming here."

She passed Gran the scissors. Her hands were as jittery as her voice.

Gran inspected the wool sock. "Is there now?" she

said as she smoothed the toe. "For Aloysius, I expect."

Patsy hopped about like a hiss of water on a hot stove. "Should I go tell them that Uncle's not home?" She started for the door.

"No, no," Gran replied.

Gran didn't understand. Patsy blurted, "One of them has a suit on, and he's carrying a satchel."

With a start, Gran looked up. Patsy could almost see her hackles rise. Gran prised herself out of the rocking chair and hobbled to the window, favouring her hip. "The nerve...." she muttered. The room was charged with her fury. She bustled to the door, massaging her hip as she went.

Patsy was right on her heels.

Gran had the door open before the men reached the porch stoop. "And what might ye be after?" she snapped, her voice brittle as pothole ice.

The government man blabbered, "Good evening, Mrs. Fitzpatrick. A grand evening, isn't it? If you don't mind, I'd like to have a few words with you."

Gran fumed. "I do mind. I have nothing to say to the likes of ye."

The government man, all set to blabber some more, was about to set foot on the stoop, but the one Maggie had called Syl Pardy grabbed his arm. "We'll be off then," Syl said, bobbing his head at Gran.

Gran sent him a withering look. "Your grandmother would turn in her grave if she knew what ye're mixed up with."

Syl slunk away.

The suit man puffed himself up for another try. He reached into his satchel and took out a paper.

"Let me give you this letter…to make sure you have the right information."

Gran closed the door in his face.

Patsy waited until Gran had gone back to the kitchen. Then she opened the door and called out, "Sleeveens."

Syl Pardy looked back.

With all the disgust she could muster Patsy spat, "Government Pardy." Then she slammed the door. She felt quivery.

In the kitchen, Gran hunched over the stove. The black dress was slack on her shoulders. She must have lost weight since she'd bought it. Her hand gripped the lifter as if she were about to raise the lid to put in some wood. But the stove wasn't lit this evening.

Patsy touched her grandmother's arm. The loose flesh of Gran's upper arm wobbled. "Gran? Are you okay?"

Gran straightened up and smoothed a few loose strands of hair as if she were shaking off whatever ailed her. "Indeed I am okay," she said. "It'll take more than them two upstarts to frighten your Gran into her grave."

Patsy smiled. Gran was back to her old self.

"What about a bite to eat?" Gran asked. "You must be starved. I can heat up some supper for you, if you like."

Patsy didn't feel like supper, though she was hungry, she realized. Instead, she devoured two slices of home-made bread and Gran's bakeapple jam. "Do you want me to wash up my dishes, Gran?"

"That'd be nice, dear," Gran said. Her smile didn't make it to her whole face. She sat in the rocking chair tracing the purple ridges of veins in her hand. "Then would you like to come up to the attic with me?"

"Sure," Patsy said. She'd never been in an attic! She put away her dishes and hung the dishtowel on the hook by the cupboard. "I'm ready," she said, curious to see Gran's attic. "What's up there, Gran?"

The grim look faded from Gran's face. "Oh, a bit of everything," she said. She picked up the wool socks she'd just finished and eased herself out of her chair.

Patsy bobbed behind her up the stairs, across the landing, and then up another narrower set of stairs, wide enough for only one person. She waited behind Gran's black dress and wrinkled stockings for Gran to lift up the square of board in the ceiling.

Gran stepped inside. Patsy stood on the last step, poked her head through the opening, and peered up at the slanted roof. She'd read about attics, cluttered ones where all kinds of things were stored. There was lots here to be sure, but everything was neat and clean. Gran tidied her attic like she did her kitchen.

Hooked rag mats were scattered over the wooden floor. Old fashioned oval-framed pictures of men wearing mustaches and women in long dresses hung on the walls. A framed hanging done in needlework read: Dare To Do Right.

Patsy counted five trunks along the walls. There was also a rocking chair with a rose-coloured cushion and back rest.

Gran sat in the rocking chair next to one of the trunks. She opened the lid and laid the socks she had just finished inside.

Patsy knelt by the trunk. "Why are you putting the

~73~

socks in there?" she asked. It was full of Gran's knitting – big gloves and mitts, stocking caps, socks and vamps in greys, blacks, and browns.

Gran rearranged some of her handiwork before she replied. "They're for Aloysius. So he'll be looked after when I go."

The setting sun flashed through the undersized window onto the metal of the raised trunk lid. Patsy couldn't look at Gran. Neither of them spoke. Patsy was thinking about the cemetery. Maybe Gran was too.

Earlier, Patsy had decided not to mention the cemetery to Gran. Now, as suddenly as the shaft of light was there and gone, Patsy changed her mind. She heard herself say, "Gran, when we were at Collins' Cove we went to the cemetery."

Gran turned the wedding band on her finger. Patsy waited for her to say something.

But all Gran said was, "Oh?"

Patsy went on. "Loretta said you wanted to be buried with Grandfather. Is that why you want to stay in Shoal Harbour?"

Gran didn't answer her question. Instead she said, "What did you think of Collins' Cove? Do you have a place like that to swim back home?"

"Not like Collins' Cove. It's really pretty there. But we have Salmon Hole. It's a big hole in the river and it's surrounded by flat rocks to lie on and a huge rock to dive off. And one end of the hole is really deep and the other end is shallow, for kids who don't swim so well. I always swim in the deep end." Gran wouldn't mind if she bragged a bit.

Gran nodded as she listened. "And how do you like

Maggie and Loretta?"

"They're really nice. I wish Jeanette could meet them. She's my best friend." Patsy sat back on her heels.

"Do you miss her?"

Patsy nodded. "I think about her lots, even when I'm playing with Loretta and Maggie. But I'll be home again next week."

Like a storm-size wave it hit her, surging all through her body. "Oh, Gran," she sobbed, laying her head in Gran's lap. "You shouldn't have to leave your home...and all your friends...."

Gran stroked her hair. "Don't you fret. 'Twill be a dreary place if everyone gets down in the mouth now, won't it?"

Patsy's sobs quieted. She lifted her head and wiped her eyes with the back of her hand. "I got your dress all wet."

Gran patted her shoulder. "Never mind," she said. "The baby does worse."

Patsy tried to smile, but she knew it was a poor excuse for one.

Gran stood up and crossed the room to a wooden trunk against the wall.

Curious, Patsy followed. She watched as Gran opened it and took out a paper bag. She closed the lid of the trunk and sat on it before removing a wad of tissue paper from the bag. Patsy sat next to her, eyes on the paper. "What is it, Gran?"

"It's for you, if you like it," Gran said, peeling back the layers.

Patsy waited. Her fingers itched to get at the tissue

paper. Gran unwrapped the last layer.

Patsy drew in her breath. "O-o-o-oh, Gran," she said, "it's so beautiful!"

An emerald-green Christmas ball the size of a small cabbage lay in her lap. Gran held it up by its string, and Patsy saw her reflection in its shimmer. "Can I hold it?" she asked, awe in her voice.

Gran passed it to her. "Be careful now. Right nish, that is."

Patsy nodded. She cradled the shimmering glass ball in her hands. "Where did you get it, Gran?"

"Your grandfather brought it to me when he came back from his first trip to St. Pierre just after he got the schooner. That was the year 1907." She paused. "We were only married a year."

Patsy cupped her hands carefully around the fragile ornament and passed it back to Gran. For a moment Gran's eyes seemed to look beyond the attic walls. Patsy waited for her to return to her story.

Gran's thumb caressed the emerald ball. "It was close to Christmas when he brought it, and every Christmas since then the ball has hung in the front room. Next to the Christmas tree."

"Are you sure you want to give it away, Gran?" Patsy asked. Her eyes lingered on the reflection of Gran's face in the ball.

At that moment Uncle Wish's head popped inside the attic. "I thought I heard someone up here. What are ye doing in the gloom?"

Gran wrapped the ball in its tissue paper cocoon. "I'm giving Patsy the Christmas ball," she said.

Uncle Wish stayed where he was, half in and half out

of the attic. He didn't move a muscle. When he finally spoke, his voice was strangled. "Mother, is everything okay? You're not feeling poorly, are ye?"

Gran looked at him sharply. "I'm fine, my son. Don't you worry." She tut-tutted as she put the ball gently back in the bag.

Uncle's whole body relaxed. At least the half of him Patsy could see did. His face was wreathed in smiles when he looked at Patsy. "Well, in that case," he said, "I couldn't think of a better one to give it to."

Patsy forced her lips to smile back. The smile wouldn't come by itself, because she knew why Uncle had looked so anxious. Jeanette's grandmother gave Mrs. Eileen her good purse and the family Bible before she died.

But Gran wasn't sick. She was fine. She said so.

10. Dinghy For Sale

Saturday! And Uncle Wish had said they would go shopping – in Beachy Cove!

Patsy's face dropped when she looked out the window. The whole harbour was wrapped in fog.

Uncle Wish saw her dismay. "Pay it no mind," he said. "It'll be long gone 'fore Dora and Mae are set to go."

By twenty past nine, Patsy was ready. The only one ready. Tired of being told "later" every time she asked when they were leaving, she'd come outside to wait. She sat with her feet hanging over the stagehead and kicked her heels against the sticks nailed like a ladder across the front. With each impatient thought, she kicked harder and faster. Finally, with legs tired and heels hurting, her feet hung just above the water at high tide.

"How come it takes grownups so long to get ready to go anywhere?" she asked a seagull circling overhead. "Hurry up," she called back to the house, mimicking a fed-up adult tone. "I'm sick and tired of this waiting."

Uncle Wish's dory was moored in a grey blur. She could barely make it out. The rest of the harbour was cut off completely, like the world ended in the ghostly nothing past Uncle's dory.

Patsy threw back her head and breathed a deep, damp breath. She giggled. It was almost like breathing and drinking at the same time! She liked fog. She liked its misty coolness on her face. And she liked the way it made her feel inside, like a rest after a day or two of busy sunshine.

She decided to see how far she could lean without falling in. At the sound of Uncle Wish's rubber boots crossing the rough stage she bobbed up quicker than a startled partridge.

"How'd you like to earn your keep?" Uncle Wish asked, lifting the mooring rope.

"Sure!" Patsy jumped up. She slipped on the wet wood but caught herself before falling.

"Take your time. You'll be no help if you break a leg," Uncle Wish teased.

Patsy blushed. Uncle Wish let her pull the rope to bring the dory in. Patsy's proud grin as she pulled the boat alongside the stage was bright enough to burn away the fog.

Uncle Wish climbed down and held his hand up to her. "Take it easy," he cautioned. "It's a mite slippery."

Patsy picked her steps. She didn't want Uncle to see her slip again. He might think she had the brain of a squid and wouldn't want her help. With her hand in Uncle Wish's tight grip, she stepped on the gunnel. The dory hardly moved under her weight.

"Did you already go fishing this morning, Uncle?" Patsy asked, as she jumped down.

"Yep. 'Fore daylight." Uncle Wish gathered some nets, a rope, a blackened kettle, and his oil clothes. "I want you to pass these to me," he told Patsy. He climbed up to the stagehead.

Patsy did as she was told. Then she sat on a thwart to wait for him to return.

"So there you are!"

She looked up to see Loretta peering down. "I went to the house, but your mom said you were out here. I couldn't see you anywhere, maid." Loretta carried a raincoat. She stuffed a paper into the pocket.

Patsy climbed up to join her. "I was helping Uncle Wish get the dory ready," she said.

"Maggie can't go," Loretta informed her. "No room."

"Oh," Patsy said. She hadn't seen Maggie since they'd parted yesterday.

"She gets to help Mom babysit Florence Anne," Loretta told her.

"Do you go to Beachy Cove often?" Patsy asked.

"Maybe once a month. We buy about half of our groceries here and the rest in Beachy Cove. It's a bit cheaper there, but Mom says Miss Martha needs the business."

A loud thump, then another one, came from inside the house. The girls looked. The front door creaked open. Aunt Dora and Mom stepped out onto the stagehead.

Loretta covered her mouth to hide a giggle.

"What are you laughing at?" Patsy asked.

"Only time the front door is used is for funerals, to

~80~

bring out the coffin." Loretta's voice was low.

Patsy giggled with her.

Uncle Wish had come up behind them. "These two look pretty much alive to me," he said, sending a grin in the direction of the front door.

Aunt Dora and Mom traipsed across the stage wearing raincoats. Mom passed Patsy hers. "Put this on over your jacket," she said. "It'll be cold out in the bay."

Patsy didn't protest. Everyone else was bundled up.

She was surprised at how nimbly Mom and Aunt Dora boarded the dory. Uncle Wish told them to sit in the stern. "For ballast," he said, winking at the girls.

Patsy and Loretta squeezed together in the bow.

The engine sputtered and caught. They were off! Patsy hugged her knees in anticipation. Her first ride in Uncle Wish's dory, and it would be a long one too! She waved to Gran who stood in the door tugging her black sweater around her shoulders.

As they neared the harbour centre, Uncle Wish called, "Care to stop for a swim?"

Patsy wrinkled her nose at him.

She felt the dory turn toward the Point, the huge headland at the harbour entrance. Today it wasn't very pointy, with most of its massive bulk shrouded in fog. But Patsy knew it was there, obscure behind the fog as an iceberg beneath the water's surface.

She closed her eyes to hear and feel the putt-putt of the motor like a steady heartbeat and the water slapping at the bow as the dory sliced through it.

They left the shelter of the harbour. Uncle Wish opened full throttle and they rode the swells to open sea. The air turned colder and a breeze picked up.

When the dory rode a really big swell, spray zinged over them.

Patsy and Loretta huddled low in the bow. Their eyes peeped over the gunnel. Mom and Aunt Dora had their hoods up and gloves on. Patsy grinned at their wet faces. Uncle Wish too had his collar up. Patsy jammed her cold hands deep in her pockets and looked around. The motor was too noisy for chat.

The fog let up some once they were out in the bay. In the distance Patsy could see patches of blue water underneath snips of sky showing through the fog. And while the dory chugged through moody grey swells, near the shore the surface was watery green like spills of the tempera paint she used in art class.

A few minutes later, Uncle Wish throttled back and they motored into Beachy Cove. Here too the houses and stages settled next to the water, with the government wharf dominating the harbour.

Uncle Wish motored past it and cut back the engine further as he snaked around boats on their moorings – wide-bellied skiffs, buff dories, small square-ended punts, and dinghies, and even a couple of longliners boasting cabins. He tied up at one of several stages clustered together.

Patsy would have lingered to look at the boats, but Loretta called her. She ran to catch up, past coils of rope, barrels of brine and blubber, and the strong fishy smell of cod drying on flakes. They tramped around the stage and up the hill to the road.

"Watch the cars," called Mom in alarm.

Patsy and Loretta jumped to the side of the road, barely ahead of the noisy blue station wagon belching foul exhaust as it rattled by.

Uncle Wish was smart. He had stayed on the other side of the fence. He whistled as he walked along the bank and headed for a shop that looked like it could have been a fish stage at one time. The only sign out front was a rusty Pepsi ad.

"That's Mr. Rose's shop. We'll go there later," Loretta said. She and Patsy followed the road uphill. It ended among a cluster of two-story houses with peaked roofs and full clotheslines flapping in the front yard.

In front of them was a low flat-roofed building. A hand-painted sign over the door read: "Uncle Greg's Ice Cream." Inside, Uncle Greg himself scooped a strawberry cone for Loretta and a chocolate one for Patsy.

"Fair weather in the bay this morning?" Uncle Greg, who was not an inch taller than Loretta, smiled a mostly toothless smile.

"Nah, foggy," Loretta replied.

He nodded. "The Point's like a trap. Ah, ye'll have to move here to Beachy Cove. God's country."

Patsy bristled. Beachy Cove wasn't God's country. If any place was, it was Shoal Harbour.

"Well, I think we'll be scattered all over," Loretta said. "Even to Cape Breton."

"Yes, I hear the Parsons are off to Sydney." He shook his bushy head. "What about Wish and the old lady?"

Patsy glared at the ice-cream man. Gran was not an old lady. And it was none of his business where she went. She barely grunted a thank you for the cone and waited at the door while Loretta chatted with Mr. Nosy.

"They haven't decided," was all Loretta said.

Outside, Patsy still had her dander up. "Busybody old man," she sputtered.

"Ah, he was just being friendly," Loretta said. "Want to taste mine, and I'll taste yours?"

They exchanged licks and laughs. Loretta reached in her pocket for a tissue to wipe her sticky fingers. She hauled out the paper Patsy had seen in her hand on Gran's stage.

"I'd better not lose this," Loretta said.

"What is it?" Patsy asked, eyeing the folded sheet.

"It's about Dad's dinghy. I have to ask Mr. Rose to pin it up in his shop." Loretta wiped her mouth with the back of her hand. "Let's go do it."

"Good thing Maggie's not here," Patsy said, falling into step beside her.

Loretta nodded. "Mom gave it to me in the porch so Mag wouldn't see."

Poor Maggie. Patsy felt sorry for her.

They met Mom and Aunt Dora coming out of a grocery store about three times as big as Miss Martha's shop.

Patsy didn't see any groceries. "Didn't you buy anything?" she asked.

"We'll leave them here until we're ready to leave," Mom said.

"What if somebody takes them?" Patsy asked, looking back at the closed door.

"Don't be silly, maid," said Loretta. "Nobody's going to touch them. Mrs. Kane will set them next to the counter. We do that all the time."

Mom and Aunt Dora decided to stroll around Beachy Cove to see if the place had changed much.

Patsy and Loretta raced to Mr. Rose's shop. Loretta pulled a string to lift the latch and the wooden door swung in on a dim smoky room. She warned Patsy, "Watch your step."

Patsy blinked and clutched the back of Loretta's coat. After a minute or so her eyes adjusted to the gloom. She followed Loretta to the grubby counter. Even the pale square of light filtering through the dingy window at the back was grey and full of little floating specks. Patsy made a face.

Most of the shelves were empty and the rest just about. There was a plentiful supply of barrels and crates. A bunch of men, including Uncle Wish, sat on them around a red-hot, pot-bellied stove. Smoke, as heavy as the fog in the harbour this morning, hung thick over their heads. More curled upward from the cigarette or pipe each held in his mouth.

And their tempers were as hot as the stove. As far as Patsy could make out, the finger-stabbing and tongue-lashing was aimed at a red-haired fellow perched on a barrel. His back was to the counter.

"Listen, byes," he said, shrugging. "It's progress."

"I tell ye, they're aimin to sell us a parcel of lies," said the grizzled old skipper next to him, all up in arms. "Mark my words. 'Twill cause more hardship than it cures." He tapped ashes into a filthy sardine can that overflowed onto his bony knee.

Patsy's eyes smarted. She fanned the air in front of her face to clear the smoke. Resettlement talk here too. She squinted at one of the men, pot-bellied himself, who got up from an upturned crate and went behind the counter. Mr. Rose, she figured.

Mr. Rose leaned on the counter so that his head was level with Loretta's. "What can I do for you, little lady?"

"Mr. Rose, Mom wants to know if you'll put this up in your shop?" Loretta showed him the paper.

He scrutinized it. Then he looked at Loretta. "Sure, I'll do that for ye." He slid a full bottle of sweets across the grimy counter towards Patsy and Loretta. "Help yourselves to a molasses candy," he said.

Patsy's eyes met Uncle Wish's across the room. He winked at her. She smiled back and sucked her candy. She watched Mr. Rose pull a few yellowed sheets off the wall. He used one of the tacks to attach Loretta's paper.

When the red-haired fellow got up to peer over Mr. Rose's shoulder, Patsy recognized him. Syl Pardy.

Syl Pardy looked back at Uncle Wish. "They're leaving in a fortnight, aren't they?"

Uncle Wish looked past Pardy.

No one asked Uncle when he was leaving. But Patsy felt the question in the air.

Syl Pardy sat down again. "You'll be the only ones left in the Bight, you and your mother," he said.

Uncle Wish sized up the growing ash on the end of his cigarette. "I expect we will," he said, slowly and evenly. After a long moment he tapped the cylinder of ash into his rubber boot.

Syl perched on the edge of the barrel. "I heard a rumour," he said, "that you and the old lady are goin with your sisters." He lodged his heel against the iron handle on the front of the stove.

Patsy listened, mesmerized. She wished Syl Pardy

would burn the foot right off himself. Her face was as red and hot as the stove. She'd been the one who'd said that. To Maggie and Loretta. Had they told their mom? And who else? Did Uncle Wish know she was the blabbermouth? He'd be so mad if he knew. So would Mom.

Patsy stared at a spot on the canvas floor that was worn right to the boards. She was petrified Syl Pardy would say where he'd heard the rumour.

Uncle Wish stood up. He turned his back to Syl Pardy, as if he couldn't stand the sight of him. And while he snuffed out his cigarette in the sardine can on the stove he said, "That's for me to know and you to find out." Uncle Wish turned on Syl. "I will tell you one thing though." He took his time and did up his jacket. "Stay out of the Bight if ye know what's good for ye." Then he nodded to the men and said, "Well, better be getting underway 'fore the fog closes in again."

Patsy and Loretta scuttled out of Mr. Rose's shop. Uncle Wish followed them up to the road.

Patsy spied Mom and Aunt Dora walking toward them. Their arms were loaded with groceries. She took a bag and trotted ahead. She couldn't look at Uncle Wish.

Aunt Dora called, "Patsy, this way. We're taking a short-cut down the hill."

Uncle Wish pointed to a bulldozed area on his right. "You know Paddy Lundrigan over by the wharf? His boy, Neil, is moving his house here."

"Is that so?" said Aunt Dora. "When?"

"Moving what?" Patsy asked.

"The house," Uncle Wish replied.

Single file, they tramped the path around the stage. "The house!" Uncle Wish must be joshing.

"It's true," Loretta said. She passed a bag of groceries down to Uncle Wish, who stowed it under a thwart.

"How can they do that?" Patsy asked.

Uncle Wish told her. "They'll raise the house off the foundation and float it to Beachy Cove."

He didn't say much of anything after that until Patsy asked. "Why don't you float Gran's house to Cape Grande?"

There was Mom's impatient look again. And the voice to go with it. "Patsy, you just can't float a house anywhere you like."

Uncle Wish's unlit cigarette hung in the corner of his mouth. "It's not so much where to go," he said, pausing a long time before finishing, "as it is the leaving."

Then he started the engine.

11. House on a Barge

"If you keep eating them, Mag, there won't be any to bring home." Loretta frowned at her sister before digging into her can to remove a tiny leaf.

"They're not ripe yet anyway," Maggie retorted. Her fingers homed in on the only two ripe raspberries on the bush. She popped one luscious berry into her mouth and the other into her can.

Patsy peered into her lard pail. The bottom wasn't covered. She was glad no one watched how many *she* ate.

"They'll probably be ripe next week," Loretta said. She stepped cautiously around the scratchy bushes and started back to the shore.

Patsy said nothing. She wouldn't be here next week. She didn't want to think about it.

She looked for the least painful way out of the tangle of brush that surrounded her. Gingerly she pushed aside a prickly limb that was too tall to step over. Underneath was the biggest, fattest raspberry she'd ever seen! When she bent to pick it, the berry rolled into her hand. "Hey, Maggie, look at the whopper I found!" She high-stepped the last bush.

Maggie waited for her. "Oh, Patsy, can I have it? I'll let you row all the way back."

Patsy grinned. "Okay." She'd have given it to Maggie anyway. She felt this was her peace offering. Maggie hadn't mentioned their fight at the cemetery, but it niggled Patsy still.

Maggie popped the plump berry into her mouth. She rolled her eyes and pretended to swoon.

Patsy caught her, and they collapsed in gales of laughter on a grassy mound.

Patsy was the first to struggle to her feet. Anxious for her chance to row home, she picked up her can and shoved Maggie's at her. "C'mon," she said, "or Loretta will leave us here."

When they reached the beach she stopped short. "Oh, no!"

Loretta laughed at her consternation. "What's the matter? Low tide, that's all."

It sure was. The dinghy sat on the strand in no more than an inch of water. "We should put wheels on the 'Bay Boy' for when the tide is out," Patsy said, straining as she helped push the boat to deeper water.

Once the "Bay Boy" was afloat, the girls hopped aboard. Maggie perched on the bow as usual, with Loretta in the stern. Patsy slipped the oars between the tholepins.

"Look," said Loretta, pointing. "There's a barge just off the Point."

Maggie wheeled around to see. "They're moving

Neil's house today. I heard Uncle Wish tell Mom." Her voice was flat.

Loretta shaded her eyes and looked across the harbour. "Yep, there's a crowd there already."

Patsy shaded her eyes too for a look. "Could we go over there?" If a house was going to be moved, she wanted to see it. Wouldn't that be something to tell Jeanette!

Maggie sent her a deadly look. "Why would you want to go and gawk at someone's house being torn down?"

"It's not going to be torn down, Mag, you know that," said Loretta. "They're moving it, that's all."

Maggie laced into her sister. "That's all, is it? Well, let me tell you something, Loretta Farrel. It's the same thing to me. Neil's house won't be here anymore, will it?"

Loretta sighed. "Let's go, Patsy," she said.

Patsy no longer needed help with rowing. She bit her lip in concentration, lined up the oars, and dipped them cleanly in the calm of Mooring Cove. There wasn't a ripple, not a breath of wind to stir a wrinkle on the water.

Inside the dinghy, there were plenty of ripples. Maggie's chin stuck out like a rock ledge. Loretta, determined either to be pleasant or to irritate Maggie further, hummed a little ditty. Patsy wished she would shut up and was glad when Maggie told her to.

Patsy had never rowed this distance. Her arms were tired and her muscles ached. Twice she slapped the oars clumsily on the water. No one laughed.

Finally, they passed Gull Rock. Just about there. As they neared shore, Loretta spotted her mother crossing the yard to Gran's house. "There's Mom," she said. "Tie up at Uncle Wish's stage."

Patsy pulled in the oars. While not quite as expert as

the girls, she thought she did a decent job of guiding the dinghy alongside the stage.

Maggie tied up.

Careful not to upset their cans, they scrabbled one-handed up to the stagehead. One by one they straggled into the house. Patsy shook her can to plump up her single layer of berries.

Maggie and Loretta plunked their pails on the table.

"Well, are the raspberries ripe yet?" their mom asked. She tipped the cans to peer inside.

"Not yet," Maggie replied. "Maybe next week."

"Mag and Patsy ate most of theirs," Loretta said, taking a berry from her sister's can and putting it into Florence Anne's outstretched hand.

"I'm not surprised that Mag ate hers or Patsy either, for that matter," said Aunt Marion. "Remember Mae, Dora?"

The two women looked at Mom who laughed with them.

"I may have eaten a lot of berries," Mom said with a wink at the girls, "but I picked two cans to your one."

"You did have the knack," Aunt Marion agreed. She emptied the contents of Maggie and Loretta's cans into Patsy's. "We'll leave these for Gran."

"Where is Gran?" Patsy looked at Mom.

The teasing girlish look faded from Mom's face. "She had a headache and went to lie down for a spell," she said, wiping Florence Anne's hand with a tissue.

"That's odd," said Maggie. "Gran doesn't usually lie down in the middle of the day."

"Mom," Loretta said, "they're moving Neil's house today. Can we go watch? We won't get too close."

Maggie flounced out the door muttering to herself.

Aunt Marion didn't reply right away. "Well, they got a good day for it," she said. She rubbed her earlobe. "I mind when I used to babysit Neil before I was married."

"And now I babysit Neil's little one," Loretta added. "At least I did. Guess I won't any more."

Patsy felt guilty about Maggie. But she desperately wanted to see the house-moving. Eager for an answer, she shook Mom's arm. "Can I go, Mom? I've never seen a house being moved. Can I?"

Mom looked at Aunt Dora and Aunt Marion like she didn't quite trust herself to make the right decision. "I suppose it'd be okay, do you think?"

Aunt Dora nodded. "I think so," she said. "Wish is there, but don't go bothering him. He'll be busy."

The girls were out the door before their mothers remembered it was lunchtime.

Loretta ran up the hill. Patsy called after her, "You go ahead. I'm going to see if Maggie will come."

"Good luck!" Loretta yelled over her shoulder.

Patsy spotted Maggie sitting on the slip. She ran down the bank. "Hey, Maggie, come with us?" She half-expected Maggie to tear into her.

But Maggie sat there savagely rubbing her eyes. She'd been crying.

Patsy sat next to her.

Maggie moved away from her.

"Well, if you don't go, I'm not going," Patsy said, scuffing her heels on the ground.

Maggie sniffed. She wiped her eyes and nose all in one motion like a cat.

"We could go see if that copper-top Syl Pardy and the government man are there and throw rocks at them or push them down the hill or something," Patsy joked, grinning at her foolishness.

Maggie brightened up as if considering the idea. "Okay," she said, in a shaky but interested voice.

Patsy swallowed. She hadn't really meant it. But it did sound like fun! Just not the kind you'd want your mom to know about.

Maggie grabbed her hand. They ran up the hill and around the shore, not stopping until they were past the government wharf. Patsy knew where Neil's house was by the crowd standing along the road and sitting on the hillside.

There wasn't much to see at first. Most of the boards skirting Neil's two-story house had been removed. A few men, Uncle Wish one of them, worked at tearing off the few remaining pieces. Patsy thought it looked kind of naked and sad.

Everyone around her seemed to think so too. Hardly anyone spoke and when they did their voices were hushed. Patsy looked around, but was careful not to stare. Even the children seemed to have caught the subdued mood and stayed close to their mothers or grandparents. There were no dads. They were helping to move the house.

"Which one is Neil?" Patsy asked.

In answer Maggie edged to the front of the small crowd. "That's him there throwing the boards clear."

Patsy was surprised at how young he looked.

As if reading her thoughts Maggie said, "He got married last year. We went to his wedding."

Next to Patsy, two women chatted in whispery voices. "My dear, it's awful hard to see the first house going."

Her friend nodded.

Maggie whispered in Patsy's ear. "Let's stroll up the hill and see if we can see you-know-who."

Patsy followed Maggie. She spotted Loretta sitting with a group of people and waved.

Maggie yanked her arm. "Leave her be. She'll blab everything to Mom." She scanned the hillside. "Do you see them?"

Patsy checked the bystanders along the road. There was no sign of Syl Pardy or the government fella.

Maggie sat on the bank next to an old man. She pulled Patsy down next to her. "What are they doing now, Uncle Joe?" Maggie asked.

Uncle Joe chewed on a blade of grass. His eyes were fixed on the men. "Well, my dear, they'll use that big jack to raise her up."

"It's taking a long time," Patsy said.

Uncle Joe nodded. "Yes, it's a big job." He looked at Patsy. "You must be Mae's girl."

Patsy nodded.

"And how do ye like it here?"

"I love it!"

"Yes, it's a grand little place. There's lots to like." Uncle Joe gestured down the hill. "See that?"

The men were propping an end up on blocks.

The sight of it made Patsy nervous. "What if it falls?"

"They know what they're doing. Just watch."

Patsy forgot she was an outsider. Part of the waiting and watching and worrying, she drew in her breath with the others when a jack slipped and joined in the relieved chatter when the last block was in place.

"Now they'll move the skids in under." Uncle Joe

pointed to four logs the size of light poles being shoved under the house. "They're greased," he said, "so's to be easy to slide the house over them to the water."

Patsy and Maggie watched.

"Now they'll use the block and tackle to lower it on the skids. See the ropes?"

The house shifted. Its frames and sashes creaked and groaned. The anxious murmurings of family and friends were drowned out by the yells of the dozen or so men shouting back and forth.

Maggie chewed her fingernails.

Patsy knew how she felt. The print of her teeth was in her knuckles.

The house moved. Slowly, in grinding stops and scraping starts, it skidded closer to the water. The ropes were payed out one moment and held back the next.

The onlookers who had moved closer to the water's edge breathed easier. Then one of the skids hooked. For one sickening moment the house tipped.

Maggie stifled a cry. "Oh, my God!"

Patsy grabbed her hand and squeezed it tight. "Please God," Patsy prayed, "don't let Uncle get hurt. I won't even be mad if he moves to Beachy Cove. Please."

She felt Maggie tug her hand away and opened her eyes to see the house creeping toward the oversized barge secured at the water's edge by two sausage-thick ropes. "Thank you, God."

Neil's house, creaking protests, was edged onto the barge.

The barge sank low, displacing water all around it. Patsy gasped.

"It's the sudden weight. It won't sink," Uncle Joe said.

Patsy giggled. Her taut nerves relaxed. "That barge must have got a shock."

Finally, the ropes were untied. Three dories, one of them Uncle Wish's, towed the barge away from shore.

The onlookers clapped. Most wiped teary eyes. Everyone waved to the flotilla of dories and longliners escorting Neil's house out to sea.

The girls watched until the barge was well out in the harbour. "I wish we could go. We should've asked Uncle Wish," Patsy said.

"Some chance," Loretta said, coming up behind them. She gave Patsy the same superior look she often used on her sister. "He'd never let us. What if there was some trouble?" She started up the hill.

When she looked back to see if Maggie and Patsy were catching up, Maggie yelled, "You go on."

Neil's house floated away. The brown blotch below the hill where it had been looked like a festering pockmark. Nearby, a few men rolled the skids into a neat pile. For the next house, Patsy wondered?

Then she saw them. Pardy and the government fellow stood talking down by the landwash. She nudged Maggie. "There they are," she whispered. "Coopy down, so they don't see us!" She grabbed Maggie by the arm and pulled her down behind a rock.

"What should we do?" Maggie whispered back. Her black eyes shone.

"Follow me," Patsy said. She slipped behind a cluster of people. Without losing sight of Pardy and the suit man, she darted from one little bunch to another till she was as close as she dared.

Maggie was right on her heels. She stuffed her fist in

her face to stifle her giggles.

"Let's throw rocks in the water," Patsy said loudly in her most innocent voice. She picked up a good-sized one.

"Okay!" Maggie was just as loud. She picked up an even bigger rock.

They counted to three and threw. There was a wonderful splash right over Syl Pardy and the government man! Bingo!

The two whipped around. Wet to the gills they were. "What do you think you're doing?"

"Throwing rocks in the landwash," Maggie said, saucy as a crackie. "Any law against that?"

She and Patsy skedaddled then. They'd be in big trouble if Mom and Aunt Marion found out.

"Do you think anyone will tell on us?" Patsy asked Maggie. She was worried. She hadn't done anything like this before.

"I don't think so," Maggie giggled. "Did you hear everybody laugh when them two got drenched?"

Maggie swung around and looked at the harbour. "I'm glad our house is staying," she said. "Maybe we can come back for a holiday next summer and camp in our own house." Maggie grabbed Patsy's arm. "I'll write you a letter and you can come too!"

Patsy's head bobbed a yes. "For sure I'll come," she said. Then the excitement in her voice died. "I wish we didn't have to go so soon. We're leaving in a couple days. Mom has to get back to work. Aunt Dora is staying for another week."

Maggie looked at the ground. "I'll miss you."

"I'll miss you too. If Jeanette could live here and

Aunt Moira and my cousins and Mom and everybody, I'd love to live here too. I know why Gran doesn't want to leave. Everybody she knows and loves is here." She giggled and leaned on Maggie's shoulder. "Well, everybody except for me!"

Maggie laughed and gave Patsy a playful shove. "You're foolish as a loo, you know that? No, foolisher. As foolish as a tom-cod, you are!"

Patsy made a comical face. "I never heard that one before." She laughed. "How can a tom-cod be foolish?"

"He's foolish enough to hang around the wharf and get jigged," Maggie chuckled. She linked her arm through Patsy's. Her voice took on a more sober tone. "I wonder how Gran is feeling."

"I hope she won't get sick," Patsy worried aloud. She remembered Aunt Dora saying that Gran wouldn't last if she had to move. And she remembered the troubled look on Uncle's face when Gran told him she was giving Patsy the Christmas ball. Patsy's stomach was jumpy. She wished she'd never set eyes on that ball.

Gran was still lying down when Patsy got home. She didn't come downstairs the whole evening.

Patsy didn't like it. It was like when she came home from school and Mom wasn't home. The house seemed so empty.

Gran's kitchen was empty without her too, no matter how many people sat around.

After supper she snuck away to the bedroom and dug the Christmas ball out of the suitcase. She tiptoed up to the attic and put the ball back in the trunk. If Gran was going to be sick, she didn't want that old ball, no matter how beautiful it was.

12. Up the River

"Pat...sy! Pat...sy!"

Patsy sat straight up in bed. She wasn't dreaming. That was Gran's voice! She must be feeling better today! Wide awake before her feet touched the cool canvas floor, Patsy yelled, "I'm up, Gran."

She bounded across the landing. Why was Gran calling her? No one had wakened her any other morning. She'd slept until she woke on her own.

Gran stood on the bottom step. She looked tired and pale. Could it be the light in the hallway? Patsy called down. "Are you feeling better, Gran?"

Gran peered up at Patsy. "Do I look like someone who's feeling poorly?" She leaned on the railing, Patsy noticed.

As Gran talked, Florence Anne crawled past her. The baby was on the fourth step before Gran grabbed the straps of her corduroy overalls. Florence Anne screamed her annoyance.

Looking flustered by the baby's fussing, Gran called

up to Patsy, "Time to get up. We're going up the river."

Patsy rubbed her eyes. "Where's up the river?"

"You'll see," Gran said. "Get dressed and come have your breakfast."

Patsy lost no time in getting back to the bedroom. She pulled on shorts and top and ran to the bathroom to give her face what Mom would call a cat's lick.

In the kitchen, Aunt Dora packed food to take with them. Patsy sat at the table with a slice of toast and raspberry jam. "Who's going?" she asked.

"Everyone." Aunt Dora's glasses had slipped down on her nose. She looked at Patsy over the rims. "Mom, Wish, me and the baby, you and your mom, Marion and the girls."

"Where is Mom?"

"Helping Wish spread the fish to dry. They should be just about done."

"But we can't all fit in Uncle's boat, can we?"

"Hughie's taking his dory as well," Aunt Dora told her. "He's taking supplies up to Fern and Gert. It's Fern's birthday today too."

"Who's Hughie?" Patsy asked. "And Fern and Gert?"

"Hughie fishes with Wish. Fern and Gert are his sisters," Aunt Dora told her. To Gran, she said, "How old would they be now, Mom?"

Gran didn't need to think. "Fern's my age, seventy-four, and Gert's two years younger. They still spend most of the summer up the river." She looked at Patsy. "And they're as good as any man at handling a boat and roughing it."

"What do they do up there?" Patsy asked.

Gran laughed. "Now what do you think? They fish,

pick berries and the like. Been doing it for the better part of their lives."

Mom had come in while Gran was talking. "Who's that? Fern and Gert?"

Gran nodded. "I mind when their mother, Mrs. Nellie, died," she said. "I can still see them clinging to their dad, one on either side of him like burrs stuck to his sleeves."

"How old were they?" Mom asked.

"Fern was twelve and Gert ten. Their father raised them the best he knew how. And they wouldn't have it any other way."

"Does Fern still smoke?" Aunt Dora asked.

"Indeed she does. Like a tilt." Gran shook her head and chuckled. "She won't listen to any talk of slowing down either."

Patsy smiled. If Fern and Gert could make Gran laugh again, she couldn't wait to go up the river!

Mom looked intently at Gran. "Are you sure you're up to going, Mother? I can stay back with you, you know. I don't mind."

Mom was carrying on worse than she did when Patsy caught the sniffles. Patsy half expected any minute she would up and feel Gran's forehead.

"My dear, I tell ye I'm fine," Gran said, plastering a bright smile on her face. "Now quit your fussing and let's pack up."

Aunt Dora, with the baby bundled in her arms, walked over to join Aunt Marion and Loretta in Hughie's boat. Maggie would ride with Patsy in Uncle's dory.

Uncle Wish and Mom hovered over Gran as she

climbed down into the dory. With everyone settled in their places, Uncle Wish started the motor.

Gran squeezed Patsy's hand and winked at her. Patsy squeezed back. Gran was just as pleased to be going as she was.

Uncle Wish guided the dory away from the stage and steered right along the coastline. Hughie followed at a distance. They rounded a point of land and could no longer see houses.

When the dory cruised past the headland near the cemetery, everyone crossed themselves and said a prayer. Maggie nudged Patsy and pointed to Collins' Cove. Only a sliver of beach remained. The rest was swallowed by high tide. But the meadow was a patch-work of colour.

A few minutes later, Uncle Wish cut back the motor. Patsy craned her neck to see around him. Uncle bore left in a wide arc and there was the river, so wide and fast Patsy's eyes boggled. She couldn't sit still.

Maggie gave her a good poke and yelled in her ear. "Stop rooting around. I'll be black-and-blue before we get there, maid!"

They entered the mouth and traveled upstream. The dory bucked and fought the fast water. The engine's chug-chug was noisy and grew noisier. Patsy loved it! She grinned at the water, the shoreline, and at whoever happened to catch her eye.

The brisk current grew louder and rougher. Uncle Wish shouted to Mom above the din, and she motioned for Patsy and Maggie to sit on the bottom of the dory.

Patsy tried to kneel on one knee so that she could

see better, but Maggie pulled her down. "We're going through the rapids," she yelled in Patsy's ear.

Patsy's eyes all but popped out of their sockets. No one had told her about this! She wasn't afraid though, not with Mom and Uncle Wish and Maggie in the dory with her. The tumble of frothing, foaming, fast water rocked and buffeted the dory. Breathless, Patsy arched her back to get rid of a nervy sensation wiggling up her spine like a cold, wet tail fin.

Uncle Wish cut the motor and raised it out of the water. Patsy watched his every move. He stood up and poled the dory around dangerous rocks. The bumpy water tumbled past, jostling the boat as it shoved by. Patsy craned her neck to see but, under Mom's watchful eye, she didn't try to get up.

She felt the water settle into a smoother, tamer rhythm. The rapids were behind them.

Gran's lively eyes swept the breadth of the river, alert to every sound and movement.

Mom strained to see around the bend. There was a look of expectancy on her face. She nudged Patsy and pointed. In the distance was the waterfall Mom had told her about! And so big, higher than a house or maybe two houses!

Uncle guided the dory toward the rocky shore. Hughie was right behind him.

Patsy couldn't wait to get closer. Unable to drag her eyes away from the sight of the waterfall, she missed the hand Uncle held out to her and stepped in the river when she jumped out.

Maggie laughed so hard that Patsy did the same.

Mom helped Gran out.

Uncle and Hughie hauled the dories almost out of the river and tied up to a dwarf spruce. On the bank above them was a big canvas tent the same buff colour as Uncle's dory.

Two figures waded downstream. They stopped and leaned their fishing poles against a rock. They wore matching hip waders, Patsy noticed.

Mom and Aunt Dora went to meet them. They hugged and chatted for a few minutes and wished Fern a happy birthday. Then Fern and Gert strode towards Gran.

Patsy saw Gran's face light up as she greeted her old friends. Even her wrinkles seemed to smile. Gran introduced Patsy. "These are your Gran's oldest and dearest friends," she told Patsy, her hand still on Gert's arm. "We've been friends for seventy odd years, since we were old enough to talk."

Fern nodded. "And Gert hasn't stopped yet," she said. A cigarette hung from the corner of her mouth.

Patsy tried not to stare, but it wasn't easy to take her eyes away from the two spry old women, dressed like men except for the bandanas tied under their chins.

When the grownups walked toward the campsite to visit, Patsy swung her arms around Maggie and Loretta's shoulders. "Let's go see the falls!"

They scrambled after the adults to ask permission.

"Don't get too close. It's dangerous," said Aunt Marion. "And stay together."

As the girls drew near the falls, the size of the rocks lining the riverbank increased steadily. They picked their way around monstrous boulders until they were halfway up the falls. The rumble of water hurling against sheer rock drowned out their voices. Loretta motioned that they shouldn't go any closer. Neither Maggie nor Patsy argued.

They sat on a huge rock, shielded from the brunt of the hurtling waterfall by another boulder in front of them. Tons of water plunged over the drop and thundered past, a hundred times wilder than the rapids. Any word that might have been uttered was whipped away on the spray and swallowed in the uproar.

Patsy had never seen anything like it! She closed her eyes and felt the pounding of the falls inside her head. She lifted her face and received a wash of mist on her skin. If Shoal Harbour was resettled, there'd be no one left to come here. A real shame.

She wondered about Fern and Gert. They didn't seem to be worried about what was happening to Shoal Harbour.

In her mind Patsy saw Gran's face, so full of vim and vigour as she chatted and laughed with her old friends. Would Gran get her headache back when the visit with Fern and Gert was over?

Patsy jumped when Maggie poked her ribs and shouted in her ear that it was time to go back. She hated to leave the falls and turned back again and again for one last look.

Supper preparations were well under way in front of the canvas tent. A fire blazed in a circle of blackened rocks and a huge pot of boiling salmon hissed and steamed. Patsy loved a boil-up, even if it was just tea with bread and molasses when they went berry picking. But a salmon boil-up! She loved salmon!

Gert used a twig to hook a second pot off the fire.

She poked at the contents with a fork. "The potatoes are done," she said. "And I'm pretty sure the salmon is too."

Hughie used a glove to lift the pot. He drained some water off before carrying it to the rough wooden table.

Maggie set a stack of plates on the remnant of faded oilcloth half covering the table, while Loretta put out cutlery. Mom, Aunt Dora, and Aunt Marion slipped around each other piling food on whatever would hold it. Pickles, mustard, beets, buns and butter, bottled strawberries, canned peaches, date squares, and thumbprint cookies filled every square inch.

Fern laid chunks of salmon on the pot lid and peeled away the skin before setting it on a plate.

Gert set the potatoes down on the corner of the table where there was no oilcloth. She caught Patsy's eye. "Isn't this a grand scoff!"

Patsy nodded in agreement. Her mouth watered.

"It's ready," Gert announced.

Patsy filled her plate after Mom took up a sizeable chunk of salmon for her. She sat next to Maggie and Loretta on a flat rock not far from the fire.

Uncle Wish and Hughie hunkered down on stumps right at the table. "To be close to the grub," teased Fern.

Gran sat on a real chair at the table. "Guest of honour," Fern decreed. And Mom, Aunt Dora, and Aunt Marion, along with Fern and Gert, sat around in a circle on whatever they could find.

Patsy took her first bite of pink, flaky salmon. She swooned like Maggie had done with the raspberry and almost upset her plate.

Maggie and Loretta laughed.

"This is the best salmon I ever ate," Patsy declared, going back for more.

Mom levered another chunk onto her plate. "Be sure to eat your bun and potatoes too."

Supper lasted a long time. When the eating slowed down, talking picked up. Easy talk it was, gentle teasing and remembering. Patsy and the girls leaned against their rock, content to listen to the stories.

The fire died. Uncle Wish and Hughie finished off the last date squares. Right when they declared they were stuffed and couldn't eat another bite, Aunt Marion went to the dory and brought back a cardboard box.

She lifted out a chocolate cake, which she laid in Fern's lap. Aunt Dora started singing, "Happy Birthday to you…." Everyone joined in.

Patsy saw Gran sneak a finger to her eye and wipe a tear. Patsy sang louder so no one would notice that Gran had stopped singing. She slipped her arm through Gran's.

Gran held her hand tight, even when everyone clapped for Fern.

"We should have brought some candles," Loretta said.

"My dear, there's not enough candles in Shoal Harbour," Fern laughed. She wiped a knife and cut big slices for everyone.

Fern hugged Gran and said something in a low voice before she passed her some cake. Patsy's ears perked up, but she couldn't hear. It must have been good though, because Gran smiled at Fern and nodded. After that Gran's whole self perked up and she ate all her cake.

Finally Gert said, "Well, let's get the dishes done."

But Mom had already organized the cleanup. "Me and Dora and Marion will do the dishes. The girls can look after the baby. And you and Mom and Fern can take it easy," she informed Gert.

Uncle Wish and Hughie disappeared up the river with fishing poles in hand.

Patsy spied Gran walking with Fern and Gert toward the tent. She hoped they would say something to Gran to make her feel better. She didn't want Gran to be sick again tomorrow.

A while later Uncle Wish and Hughie returned. Without a salmon. "Are they still in there?" Uncle Wish asked.

"Not a sign of them since you left," Mom told him.

"I wonder what they're talking about?" Maggie said.

Patsy shrugged. Her eyes wandered to the tent again and again.

Finally the three friends emerged. Patsy studied Gran's face but couldn't read her expression.

"Well," said Uncle Wish, setting his teacup on the table, "it's time we were going."

The dories were loaded for the trip home. Patsy looked back at the falls one last time and then one very last time from the boat. The evening air was filled with good-byes that echoed across the water until the dories rounded the bend.

The sun had all but disappeared behind the hills by the time Uncle Wish tied up at the stage. Maggie ran to meet Hughie's dory while Patsy helped carry things into the house. She helped Mom and Gran put everything away while Aunt Dora got the baby ready for bed. Then Gran put the kettle on for a cup of tea.

While the adults sipped, Patsy nibbled on a tea biscuit. She wasn't hungry, but she had to do something while she waited. Gran hadn't mentioned a single word about her chat with Fern and Gert.

Dusk darkened the windows and sifted across the kitchen, but no one made a move to light the lamp.

Finally, Gran spoke. "I had a good talk with Gert and Fern," she said.

Everyone waited.

Uncle's cigarette smoke drifted with the dusk.

Gran's needles clicked in time with the clock on the stove. She finished the round on the pink sweater she was knitting for Florence Anne, then laid it on her lap and leaned forward in her chair. "They're not leaving," she announced with gumption. "And neither am I."

Silence swirled around the room like a brewing storm, stirring up troubled thoughts and unasked questions. Incredulous, concerned eyes fell away under Gran's steady gaze.

Aunt Dora was the first to find her voice. "What do you mean, Mom, they're not going?"

"They'll have to," Patsy's mom said. "Everybody else will…."

Gran put up her hand to shush them. "Fern says they don't have to. In order to shut everything down seventy-five percent of the people have to agree to move. Syl Pardy hasn't been broadcasting that, has he?" she said, with a bite to her words. She paused and massaged her hand. "Well, there's lots here that don't want to move."

Mom looked at Uncle Wish. He sat on the edge of his chair. "How many do you think want to stay, Wish?"

Gran said. "More than a quarter of us, I'd say."

Uncle Wish nodded in agreement. He began to count off people. "There's Hughie, and the Lundrigans, and the Goulds, and the Davages…."

Gran interrupted. "Fern and Gert are coming in on the weekend. They're going house to house and starting up a committee to fight this. Fern says she and Gert'll take a delegation to Confederation Building in St. John's if they have to."

Gran was as lively as a spring chicken. She prated on, her eyes lit up like Christmas, about what Fern and Gert were going to do.

The more Gran talked, the more Patsy stewed. The more they all talked, the more she steamed. Finally, she walked out on them. Strolled right across the kitchen in front of them all and left.

No one noticed. No one came after her. No one cared.

She sat on the stairs, put her head on her arms and sobbed big silent sobs. Gran and Uncle Wish wouldn't be leaving. For sure. She knew she should be happy, but she wasn't. How could she be happy when she wouldn't see Gran and Uncle Wish again for God knows how long? Maybe ever again.

But Gran didn't seem to care. Or Uncle either.

They were quite happy making their plans to stay.

And Patsy wasn't in them.

13. An In-Between Time

Patsy didn't remember falling asleep, but she must have. She opened her eyes when she felt the mattress sag. It was still dark. Mom sat on the edge of the bed, hauling on long pants.

Patsy scrambled to her knees. "Where're you going?"

"Sh-sh, don't wake the house. I'm going fishing with Wish."

Patsy, tangled in sheets, tumbled to the edge of the bed. "Me too. I'm going."

"Patsy, it's four-thirty in the morning. Go back to sleep. I'll be home by the time you get up."

"I want to come with you," Patsy said, as she tugged a sweater from the drawer.

Before Mom could argue, there was a light tap on the door. "Mae," Uncle Wish called softly, "are ye awake?"

Patsy hopped over Mom's legs and peeped around the door. "I'm awake too, Uncle. Can I come?"

Uncle looked surprised. A slow grin spread across his face. He nodded. "You're your mother's daughter, you are."

Patsy was downstairs before Mom. She wasn't going to chance being left behind. They had a quick breakfast of rolls and tea. Uncle's dishes were already in the sink.

He was in and out of the house while they finished eating. "I packed some grub," he said, on his way out. When he came back, he told Mom, "Make sure she has warm clothes." Then he came in again with a pair of rubber boots for Mom. "There's some wool socks in the porch," he said.

When Mom was fitted out, she looked like Fern and Gert, especially with the long pants she wore. Patsy recognized them as her berry picking pants. Uncle Wish looked her over and said to Patsy, "She cuts a fine figure, don't you think?"

Patsy tittered.

Uncle picked a burlap sack off the counter and passed it to Patsy. "You can carry the nunny-bag," he said.

"What's in it?" Patsy asked.

"Grub," he replied. "We'll go ashore for a mug-up."

"Great!" Patsy said. She hefted the nunny-bag to her shoulder and twirled across the kitchen to the porch.

Mom shooed her out and pulled the door shut.

The morning was a grand one. Faint light streaked the sky beyond the Point, but Shoal Harbour nestled in night yet. Not pitch black night, more like a gauzy purple-blue. There was no fog and no breeze. Not a stir. Not even a bird. Patsy looked toward Aunt Marion's sleeping house. She pitied them, missing this fine morning.

She trotted behind Uncle around the house to the

stage. Her rubbers were slick with fresh dew. She quat down, brushed her hands on the grass, and wiped her face with the magic mist. Fairy water. Her eyes, dry from last night's crying spurt, felt better.

"Patsy, what are you doing?" Mom asked from behind.

Patsy scurried across the stage.

Uncle had already pulled the dory in off its mooring and had his gear aboard. Patsy and Mom climbed down, picked their way around the anchor, Uncle's oil clothes, a coil of rope, fish tubs, and a blackened pot, and settled on the stern thwart.

As Uncle pushed off from the stage, Patsy looked at the tide line on the weathered post. She wondered if the water reached that mark every time. "Uncle Wish," she asked, "does the tide always come right up to there?"

"No, not all the time. Depends on the moon. Full moon she goes past."

"When is the next full moon?"

"Not for a spell. A few weeks."

Patsy sighed. She wouldn't be here.

Uncle started the motor. It grumbled, low and throaty, like a muttered apology for disturbing the peace.

"Isn't anyone else in the harbour going fishing?" Patsy asked.

"Gone already," Mom told her. "Cod don't wait for lie-abeds."

Patsy looked back at Shoal Harbour, caught in shades of light and dark. Between night and day. The place was snapshot-still except for the one chimney yawning smoke.

If everyone moved, that's what Shoal Harbour would become – a snapshot, a memory. There wouldn't be smoke from any chimney. No one to see any perfect morning.

She watched the water fall away in the dory's wake. The harbour, a dark bluish-grey, was as smooth as a blackboard, its calm scratched by widening ripples. Near the wharf a glimmer of light glanced off the surface.

Once past the Point the open sea was altogether different. Small scuds of wind tugged the surface, making the ride as bumpy as driving over ruts in a road.

Uncle veered left, and they putt-putted in a steady line along the zigzag coast. The motor sounded puny, its sound all but swallowed up in the bigness.

"We're almost there," Mom said.

Uncle rounded a rocky point of land and announced, "This is it. Brook Cove."

Wisps of fog drifted off the water and stuck to the woods up the shore. Two fellows on a single stage in the cove waved to them and went about their business.

"Who's that with Hughie?" Mom asked.

"Norbert, Pete-Joe's boy," Uncle told her.

Patsy spied two white buoys afloat in the cove. Uncle cut back the motor and they approached. She could see the thick black net strung underwater between the buoys.

Uncle put on his oil clothes and rubber gloves and started hauling the net hand over hand into the dory. It was heavy with water.

At the first sight of cod caught in the mesh up to its gills, Patsy was on her feet. "Look!" she cried. "Look at that!"

"You'd better sit down," Uncle Wish cautioned, "or we'll be fishin you in by the gills!"

Mom was right beside Uncle. She knew exactly what to do. As fast as he pulled the net she loosened the cod from the mesh and tossed them into a tub.

The net was full of brownish-green slime. Patsy squished back as far as she could and tucked her feet in under the thwart. Yuck! She didn't want any of it touching her.

Mom missed and a big cod landed close to Patsy's foot. Gingerly she lifted the fish to put it in the tub. Its slimy belly slipped out of her grip and slid down onto her lap. Patsy squealed and shoved it away.

Mom turned. "That won't hurt you. Just a bit of slub."

Patsy made a disgusted face and glared at the cod. "Slub. What's that?"

"Oh, scum and slime from the sea that collects on the nets."

Uncle Wish swivelled his head to see Patsy. "You're not a bayman if you haven't touched your share of slub," he said, winking at her.

The cod at Patsy's feet stared lifelessly up at her. If she was going to get rid of that stare, she'd have to sling it into the tub. She pushed up her sleeves and dug her fingers into the scummy cod skin, gripping close to the gills so it couldn't slip out of her grasp. She shuddered and slung it into the tub.

While her sleeves were up, she might as well do the same with the others. Before Mom could tell her to. Besides, she wasn't about to let Uncle think that a bit of slub made her qualmish. Soon she was racing Mom and had the fish in the tub before Mom could toss another one.

She was getting hot and reached over the side of the dory to wash her hands so she could undo her jacket.

"Look here, Patsy," Uncle said. There was a grin on his face.

Patsy edged past the slubby fish tubs to see. Tangled in the net resting on the gunnel was the weirdest fish Patsy had ever seen. "What is it?" she asked, watching Uncle remove it. It looked as if it had been flattened by a maul. A solitary eye in its middle stared up at Patsy. She stared back.

"It's a flatfish," Mom said. "A bottom fish."

"What are you going to do with it?" Patsy asked.

"How about we take it home and have it mounted?" Uncle said, straight-faced. "Wouldn't you like to have it hanging in your front room?"

Mom laughed. "I think we'll let you keep that one. You can use it for bait."

"Unless Patsy wants it for supper," Uncle teased.

Patsy made a face. "No, thank you," she said.

"There, that does it," Uncle said.

"Are we all done?" Patsy asked.

"Save for dressin and saltin," Mom said.

"How do you dress a cod?" Patsy asked, giggling.

Uncle Wish payed out the gill net.

Mom dipped her hands over the gunnel and swished them around in the water. "You see Hughie and Norbert?" she asked.

Patsy nodded.

"Well," Mom said, "they're at the splittin table, cleanin the fish and gettin them ready to be salted.

That's called dressin the fish. We'll go ashore now and you'll see."

Uncle finished with the net and rowed the dory toward shore.

The sky had lightened. Patsy wished that she had watched for it. The sun burned off the last trace of fog. The cove was bottle-glass green and just as smooth.

They tied up at a rickety old stage. Norbert came to help Uncle hoist the tubs up to the stagehead.

Patsy clambered up.

Hughie and Norbert must have been working for a while, because there were several barrels filled with salted fish.

Patsy wrinkled her nose at the salty odour.

With his sharp knife, Norbert slit the throat of a big cod and chopped the head off. Then he slid it across the table to Hughie, who split it down the middle, removed the innards, cut around the backbone, flattened the fish, and slid it into a puncheon of water at the end of the table.

"There," Mom said, "bring that to the saltin table. I'll do it for ye now."

Uncle Wish dragged the sawn-off barrel filled with cod to the other end of the stagehead. Boards laid across two barrels made a salting table.

Patsy watched Mom lay out the fish, dip salt from a puncheon with a small wooden shovel and dump it on. Then she spread it with a brush and finally with her hand.

Patsy was impressed. She hadn't known Mom could do all this. "I want to do something," she said.

"You can shovel the salt," Mom told her. "Dip up

about this much," she said, demonstrating.

While Patsy and Mom salted, Uncle started a fire on the beach.

"There, that's enough," Mom said. "I'm just about done here." She packed the cod in a barrel, layering them head to tail and dousing more salt between.

Patsy ran down to the rocky beach.

Uncle stood by the fire. The blackened pot, balanced on two rocks in the fire, contained several chunks of dried cod. The water was already bubbling.

Uncle picked up a dipper as black as the pot. "Run to the brook over there," he said, gesturing toward the grassy bank, "and get some water for tea."

Patsy heard the fast-running water before she saw it. "So this is where the name Brook Cove comes from," she said aloud. She dipped up the clear water and walked carefully back to the fire.

Mom cut thick slices of bread and lathered them with butter and molasses. "Hughie, Norbert," she said, "have some bread and lassy."

Patsy ate three slices with tea that Mom whitened with canned milk. All hands dug into the boiled cod. Patsy let her piece cool, then separated the flakes, and ate with her fingers. She licked the salt off her hand.

Mom didn't say a word about it. She was too busy chatting with Hughie and Uncle Wish. Norbert didn't say much, but he sure ate lots.

They talked about the good drying weather.

"I think now," Hughie said, "we'll bring back a couple barrels and put them out on the flakes. The forecast looks good for the next few days."

Uncle poured himself another cup of tea. He stopped, dipper in mid-air, and listened. "Do you hear that?" he asked, looking out to the cove.

Hughie threw out the rest of his tea and stood up.

"Looks like we got visitors," he said.

Mom glanced out toward the water. "Patsy," she said, "put the sugar back in the nunny-bag. Make sure the lid's on tight."

Patsy picked up the bottle. The boat coming in the cove was a longliner. She knew by the cabin on the deck.

"Looks like Syl Pardy," Hughie said. "I wonder what he's doing here?"

Patsy drew in her breath. Syl Pardy meant trouble.

The longliner eased past the buoys and came straight for them, cutting the motor a ways off shore.

It was red-haired Syl Pardy, all right. He cupped his hands to his mouth and hollered, "Hughie Lundrigan?"

Everyone gravitated to the water's edge.

"That's me," Hughie called back.

"Some bad news," Syl called. "Your sister, Fern ...she's sick. They think it's a heart attack." He paused. "Sorry to have to tell ye this way."

Mom put her hand on Hughie's arm. "How bad?" she called across the water. "Where is she?"

"She's back in Shoal Harbour. Not sure...."

Uncle Wish waved at Syl. "We're on our way."

Mom took charge. "Hughie, you and Norbert go. We'll be right behind you."

Hughie nodded. He hadn't said one word. He tore across the beach with Norbert in tow.

Patsy had a thousand questions, but there was no

point in asking any of them. Mom or Uncle Wish didn't have the answers, at least not until they got back to Shoal Harbour.

She helped Mom pack up while Uncle went back to the stage. Not a word was spoken. Finally, on the way across the beach, Patsy blurted, "What'll happen now?"

"Only God knows," Mom said. "Say a prayer for Fern."

Patsy did. She prayed all the way back to Shoal Harbour. For Fern, and Gert, and Hughie.

For Gran.

And for Shoal Harbour.

14. Baygirl

Patsy perched atop Chamber Rock. It was so big she'd had to find a toehold to climb up. She drank in every detail so she could tell Jeanette exactly how everything looked – Chamber Rock, the shingly beach, the breakers in the shallows on the far side, and the flakes. Especially the flakes.

Chamber Rock anchored the tiny beach at one end and a scraggly lone spruce, unusually tall, marked the other end.

Patsy lined up her five blue-grey beach rocks. She'd collected a whole pile, but Mom would never let her keep them all. She'd finally chosen these as her favourites, and she planned to keep them to show Jeanette. They were so rounded and smooth she couldn't stop stroking them. One by one she cradled them in her hand while she sang the song she'd made up:

> *Lots o' fish right in Shoal Harbour*
> *Lots o' cod dryin round here*

Uncle showed Patsy how to spread 'em
And she did – from 'ere to 'ere!

She was proud of her little ditty and sang heartily as she stuffed the rocks in her pocket and jumped down.

It was time to check her cod. She trudged the length of the rocky shingle, ignoring the tired pull in her calf muscles.

Uncle had given her a job. She'd come with him earlier this morning to put fresh boughs on the flakes – to let air circulate under the fish, Uncle said. Then they'd spread the cod on top to dry. A while ago Patsy had come back to turn them.

She surveyed the sky. She hoped it wouldn't rain. It had been pecking a while ago, just scattered drops. She inspected the flakes to make sure that she'd turned every single fish. Satisfied, she picked up a bough and waved it over the fish to shoo away the flies. Her fish wouldn't have any fly spit on it.

"Patsy," Mom called from the bank, "are you still down here?"

Patsy waved up at her.

Mom scrambled down. "Wish didn't mean you had to stay down here all day, you know."

"I know, but I want to."

"Aunt Dora needs you to help Gran look after Florence Anne. We're going over to see Fern."

"What about Gran? Isn't she going?"

"Gran's been over already today."

"Oh," Patsy said. "How is Fern?"

"She's coming along. She asked for a cigarette this morning." There was a fond smile on Mom's face. "But

Hughie threw them out."

Patsy chuckled. Looking after Fern would be harder than watching Florence Anne. She set her bough under the flake. "I have to come back in a while and turn my cod."

"We won't be long."

They climbed the bank to the house. "I've been washing clothes," Mom said. "We have to pack."

Patsy stopped dead in her tracks. Mom almost bumped into her. "I don't want to leave," she whined. "We just got here."

"Now Patsy," Mom said, in her trying-to-be-patient voice, "we didn't just get here. We've been here for over a week. You know I have to get back for work." In a too-bright tone she added, "We'll get to sleep on the boat overnight."

"I don't care," Patsy said. She knew she was being miserable. She didn't care about that either. Just when she was becoming a real bayman she had to leave. Actually she wasn't a bayman. She was a baygirl. While not as expert as Maggie and Loretta at rowing, she could tie up at the stage without bumping the dinghy, most of the time. And she could find a good sandy spot to beach the "Bay Boy" when they wanted to explore. She could even row halfway around the harbour without taking a rest.

But it was all over.

Mom's next words left Patsy floundering.

"Aunt Dora said you could stay until she leaves if you want."

Patsy rattled the rocks in her pocket. She hadn't expected this. Did she want to stay without Mom?

Her mother waited for an answer. "You'll have to make

up your mind fast, because I have to pack."

Patsy followed her into the porch. "Will you let me?"

"I think you should come home with me, but if you're determined to stay, I suppose you can."

The round wringer washer had been pulled into the kitchen. Its steady motor sounded like the dory and was almost as noisy. Patsy stepped over the clothes sorted in piles on the floor. She watched the water gush out as Mom fed a pair of her shorts through the wringer.

"Bring this load out to Gran while the sun's still out. Looks like it might cloud over any minute." Mom handed Patsy the clothespin bag.

Patsy picked up the oval wicker basket, heavy with wet clothes, and trudged out to the clothesline behind Gran's house. She peered up at the clouds bullying the sun out of sight.

Gran stood at the far end of the line pinning socks as high as she could reach. She turned her head and smiled at Patsy. "How's my trout?"

Patsy smiled back. "I've been turning the cod," she said. Gran seemed fine today. But the way her grandmother had looked after she'd heard the news about Fern stayed vivid in Patsy's mind. Fern really must be feeling better for Gran to be in such good spirits.

Gran broke into her thoughts. "Dora took the baby to the shop with her. I hope she remembered to put a sweater on the child." She looked up toward the road. "When the sun goes in, it's downright chilly."

"Why did Aunt Dora go to the shop?" Patsy asked.

"To send Jose a telegram so he'll be at the wharf to meet you and your mom."

Patsy frowned. She held Uncle's shirt up to the line

and stabbed it with the clothespins.

"Patsy," Aunt Dora called from the road. "Come bring the stroller down for me."

Shortly after Aunt Dora and Mom left to visit Fern, Gran put the baby down for a nap. Then she went to the front room and came back with an armful of knitting books. She set them on the table. "I'm going to knit you a sweater," she said, "and I want you to pick out the pattern."

Patsy sat on the chair next to Gran, her leg tucked under her. She looked at the covers, bright with all kinds and colours of sweaters. She saw what she wanted right away. "This one, Gran," she said eagerly. "This one with the boat on it. Except I don't want a sail. I want a dory, a yellow dory the colour of ours." She looked at Gran. "Can you knit it?"

Gran peered at the pattern. "Yes, that looks like a nice one. And what colour do you fancy for the sweater?"

"Blue. Harbour blue."

Gran chuckled. "I think I might have enough blue."

Patsy followed her to the front room where she rummaged through several bags of wool until she found the yarn she was looking for.

"Oh, Gran, that's perfect!" Patsy cooed. She hugged the soft sea-blue yarn to her.

"I'll put it up when things settle down after the summer," Gran said. "Do you want me to send it to you?"

Patsy didn't know how to answer. How else would she get it if Gran didn't send it?

Gran looked at her intently. "I'd better put it in the mail." She nodded. "If I wait...."

Patsy had a tight feeling in her chest. Did Gran mean that if she waited she mightn't be around to send it?

"If I wait until you come back next summer, you'll have outgrown it most likely," Gran said affectionately.

Then she added, "Who knows? If everything goes well with Fern, Wish and me might take it in our heads to go visit ye for a spell in the fall."

Patsy couldn't believe her ears! She hugged Gran so tight Gran grunted.

When they returned to the kitchen, Uncle Wish was there. He tweaked Patsy's plait. "How's our cod doin?" he asked.

"Good," she replied. "I'm going back to check when Mom gets home."

"There's a meeting tonight," he told Gran. "Expecting a good turnout."

"Who's calling it?" Gran asked. "Pardy?"

"No, Hughie and Gert. Hughie said it's the only way to keep Fern quiet." He poured himself a glass of water. "Did you know it was Syl Pardy who brought Fern out? He was taking some of them government fellas up salmon fishing. Left them there and came on with her."

Gran humphed. "The only decent thing to do."

Uncle didn't say anything. The silence stretched on.

Patsy mustered up her nerve. This was her chance. She had to know. She couldn't do it with Mom here. Mom would give her that look. But if she didn't ask, how was she supposed to find out? She opened her mouth, gulped, and blurted, "Gran, what if not enough people in the meeting...." She gulped again and ploughed on. "What will you do if not enough people want to stay? Where will you go?"

Gran sat in her chair, a bemused look on her face.

Uncle Wish glanced at his mother. "We'll have to decide, I figure." Then he raised his eyebrows and looked at Patsy. "Do you know anybody who'll have us?"

Patsy's heart burst with love. "We'll have ye, Uncle, me and Mom," she assured him. "And Aunt Dora and Uncle Jose will too."

"Is that so?" Uncle said in a teasing voice.

"Then there's nothing to decide." Gran roused up in her chair, but Patsy sensed it took great effort. "Where else would we go, when our folks are in Cape Grande?"

"Oh, Gran!" Patsy perched on the arm of Gran's chair. "I thought you might move to Beachy Cove!"

Gran patted Patsy's knee. "Beachy Cove? Settle in that pile o' rocks with neither hide nor hair of a relative around? No siree!"

"There's your answer," Uncle said, grinning.

The house couldn't contain Patsy's high spirits. She picked up the laundry basket with a couple of wet towels in it. "I'll hang these out for you, Gran," she offered.

Singing "Lots o' fish…." she pinned the towels on the line. She turned at the sound of Loretta racing up the bank.

"When are you leaving?" Loretta asked.

"Tomorrow." Patsy's voice went flat.

Maggie moped along behind her sister, the picture of dejection. She sat on a rock and scuffed the ground. "We'll sure miss you, maid," she said, her voice every bit as flat as Patsy's.

Loretta picked up a clothespin that had fallen on the ground. "We're leaving this week too," she announced.

"What? How come?" Patsy looked at Maggie's

forlorn face.

Loretta explained, "Mom got a telegram this morning," she said. "Dad's taking time off work. He'll be here the day after tomorrow."

Poor Maggie. She was trying so hard not to cry. Patsy couldn't think of anything to say. She recalled Loretta saying they would go back to Mooring Cove when the raspberries were ripe. Now it looked like Maggie and Loretta wouldn't get back there either.

Patsy wished they could all go once more together, and to all their other special places too, like Collins' Cove and up the river.

No wonder Gran couldn't bear the thought of leaving. Patsy had only been here a little over a week and she hated to leave.

She decided she wouldn't act miserable and get everyone down in the mouth. If anyone had a right to be miserable, it was Gran and Uncle and Maggie. But not her.

She was glad she hadn't told the girls she could stay with Aunt Dora for another week. She didn't want to be here when Maggie and Loretta's house was closed up and the "Bay Boy" pulled out of the water.

Patsy picked up the basket and took Maggie's hand to pull her to her feet.

"Got time to take out the 'Bay Boy'?" Loretta asked.

"Just a minute," Patsy said. "I'll see." She dropped the basket in the porch. Gran was in the kitchen wiping off the washer. Patsy slipped past her and made straight for the stairs. Then she skipped light as a fairy up the attic steps and inside. In a flash she had the Christmas ball in her hands. She slid the board back in place and made straight for the bedroom where she stashed the ball in the suitcase. She'd keep the ball for Gran whenever she came.

On her way out again she called, "Gran, can I go out in the boat with Maggie and Loretta?"

"Stay close to the shore," Gran cautioned. "The wind's coming up."

She ran into Mom and Aunt Dora on the stoop. "Be right there," she yelled to the girls. Patsy gave Mom a quick hug. "I'm coming home with you," she whispered.

They scrambled aboard the "Bay Boy."

Patsy leaned over the gunnel. The water mirrored the cloudy sky. She thought of the emerald Christmas ball and Gran's reflection. If Gran came to visit, she'd hang it up no matter what time of the year it was.

They pushed away from the stagehead. Maggie fitted the tholepins. Loretta slid the oars in place.

Patsy eyed the sky. More clouds bundled into the harbour from the bay and bunched up with those already on the hilltops. Wouldn't it be something if a storm came up and the steamer couldn't get into the harbour or couldn't leave? She was hopeful until she saw the sun dart through the cloud cover.

When Loretta asked if she'd like to row, Patsy shook her head. She wanted to look at Shoal Harbour one last time. She perched on the bow while Loretta rowed the dinghy away from the stage.

All of a sudden, in the middle of raising the oars, Loretta collapsed in a silly fit of giggles.

Maggie and Patsy hadn't a clue why she was laughing.

Holding the oars high in the air Loretta looked at Patsy. "Remember when you said you knew how to row?"

Patsy put on an innocent face. "Wasn't me, maid. I don't remember that."

"Sure, you did!" Loretta's eyes danced. "Well, this is for lying!" She slapped the oars down hard on the surface of the water!

Patsy and Maggie screamed as the cold spray soaked them! Water streamed down their faces. "I'll get you, Loretta!" Maggie vowed.

"Get her for me too, Maggie, and then write and tell me about it," Patsy said, laughing.

Maggie nodded. "Promise," she said. "Cross my heart." She locked eyes with Loretta until she broke out in another fit of giggles. "Now Loretta, I'm warning you, don't do that again, or I'll tell Mom."

"Okay, I won't," Loretta said. "See, the sun is out. It'll dry us in no time."

Patsy's eyes followed the shift of light. Footpaths wound in and out of sun and shadow, and grey rocks everywhere glinted silver. Roosting on the backs of the hills, like seabird nests, were the houses. She knew who lived in lots of them. Fern and Gert's, Hughie's, old Uncle Joe's, Miss Martha's shop and the house on the other side of the road where she lived with her daughter. Square and sturdy, they squeezed up against the hillsides, their painted clapboard copying the bold colours of flowers that wouldn't grow on rock.

Patsy was sure Gran's house had a special glow, that the sun, and not just her eyes, lingered there a while longer. At least it pleased her to think so. It would stay that way in her mind.

Uncle Wish called to them from the stagehead. "Hey, Skipper, come here." He beckoned to the dinghy.

Loretta rowed toward the stage.

He reached into his pocket and pulled out four tholepins.

He passed them down to Patsy. "Present for ye."

Patsy bobbed up. Her own tholepins! She shifted her weight to the side of the dinghy so fast the little boat tipped almost to the water's edge.

Maggie and Loretta squealed. Maggie grabbed the back of Patsy's sweater to keep her from tumbling overboard while Loretta shifted her weight to the other side of the boat. The "Bay Boy" righted itself.

"Patsy," Loretta laughed, "I wish you'd warn us before you do things like that."

Patsy hardly heard her. She had regained her balance, tholepins in hand. She turned to the girls. "Can we use them now?"

"Sure, but don't make any sudden movements." Loretta took two tholepins from Patsy's hand. "You do that side, and I'll do this one."

The tholepins fit snugly.

Patsy beamed. "Perfect!" she said, admiring them. When she was back home, she'd shove them right under Stella's stuck-up nose. And she'd tell Stella and the others that Uncle and Gran might not have to move away, that she hoped they could stay home in Shoal Harbour. Then she'd put her tholepins in a safe place for next summer when she came back to Shoal Harbour.

Uncle Wish had watched the operation and now winked at her. "Be careful," he cautioned with a straight face. "There's a bit of a lop. Don't get seasick."

Maggie laughed. "We won't have time to be seasick. We'll be too busy trying to keep Patsy in the boat!"

"Or from tipping us over," Loretta added.

But Patsy had the last word. She wrinkled her nose at Uncle. "Seasick?" she scoffed. "A baygirl like me?

Glossary of Newfoundland Terms

canvas – floor covering, linoleum

coopy – to squat, crouch down

crackie – small, noisy mongrel dog

dinghy – small rowing boat used in sheltered waters

dipper – cuplike container with long, straight handle used for dipping liquids

ditty – short, simple song

dory – small, flat-bottomed boat with flaring sides and a sharp bow and stern

flake – platform built on poles and spread with boughs for drying codfish

grub – food, rations for traveling

grum – gloomy, morose

loo – common loon

lop – a state of the sea in which the waves are short and jumpy

mug-up – snack, light lunch

nish – easily broken

nunny-bag – burlap or canvas knapsack

outport – coastal village

pecking – to start to rain in small drops

prate – chatter

qualmish – sensation of nausea

quat – to squat, crouch down

rory-eyed – upset, angry

scoff – a cooked meal at sea or ashore held in a party atmosphere

shingle – beach covered with small, water-worn pebbles

sleeveen – sly, deceitful person

slip – inclined plane sloping to the water

slub – brownish-green slime on fishnets

steamer – steamship, coastal boat

tilt – fisherman's hut

tom-cod – small, immature codfish

vamp – short, thick woolen sock

Resettlement

Over the years many small communities along the coast of Newfoundland were abandoned. However, beginning in the late 1950s and lasting until the early 1970s, the pace was speeded up. It was then the government developed a plan to move people from the outports. The program was a failure. Men lost their jobs in the fishery and families lost the support of their close-knit communities.

Since then some of the fishermen and their families have started returning to their outport homes seasonally to fish. The outport spirit and sense of belonging remain strong. Former residents organize reunions which bring whole communities "back home" in the summertime. In 1994, my mother attended a reunion in Bay du Nord, her former outport home, which I visited for two wonderful weeks the summer I was eleven.